DO NOT PANIC THE PIXIES

Michelle Robinson
Illustrated by
Sharon Davey

BLOOMSBURY
CHILDREN'S BOOKS

LONDON OXFORD NEW YORK NEW DELHI SYDNEY

KU-675-388

BLOOMSBURY CHILDREN'S BOOKS
Bloomsbury Publishing Plc
50 Bedford Square, London WC1B 3DP, UK
29 Earlsfort Terrace, Dublin 2, Ireland

BLOOMSBURY, BLOOMSBURY CHILDREN'S BOOKS
and the Diana logo are trademarks of Bloomsbury Publishing Plc

First published in Great Britain in 2023 by Bloomsbury Publishing Plc

A catalogue record for this book is available from the British Library

ISBN: PB: 978-1-4088-9494-1; eBook: 978-1-4088-9493-4;
ePDF: 978-1-5266-5288-1

2 4 6 8 10 9 7 5 3 1

Printed and bound in Great Britain by CPI Group (UK) Ltd,
Croydon CR0 4YY

MIX
Paper | Supporting
responsible forestry
FSC® C171272

To find out more about our authors and books visit www.bloomsbury.com
and sign up for our newsletters

For Hannah

– MR

To Neve and Alex, always

– SD

CONTENTS

1. DO NOT forget your Under-Wonders   1

2. DO NOT doubt the pixies   17

3. DO NOT use your mallet as a hammer   31

4. DO NOT count your dragons before they hatch   41

5. DO NOT be a big, snooty show-off   47

6. DO NOT be a bad sport   57

7. NEVER wang a giant welly   69

8. DO NOT give up   79

9. DO NOT trust a farting knight   85

10. DO NOT trash your own tent   97

11. ALWAYS share your problems   109

12. DO NOT panic the pixies   121

13. DO NOT invent giant slugs   137

14. DO NOT alert the leaders   147

15. NEVER lie to your parents   161

16. DO NOT lead your friends astray   169

17. DO NOT cross Chief Colossa   177

18. ALWAYS follow the leader   187

19. ALWAYS provide a perch for a pixie   197

20. EVERYONE is welcome at Questival   209

21. Golden Wonders   217

1

DO NOT FORGET YOUR UNDER-WONDERS

The dragons were unlikely to get any rest today, no matter how badly they needed it.

They'd spent the whole night flying, covering the length and breadth of the realm in search of glittering gemstones. But even now – tucked in their nests on the turrets of Wondermere Castle, the sun warming their scales – they couldn't get to sleep.

They wriggled and they shifted. They tossed and they turned. They buried their heads beneath their wings. It was no use. There was simply too much noise coming from the courtyard below.

The castle was bustling with young knights preparing for Questival. They clattered across the cobbles, loading up their unicorns with backpacks, sleeping bags, saucepans and rolled-up tents.

Questival was every young knight's first taste of questing in the great outdoors. For one wonderful weekend, they could camp under the stars and try out skills like

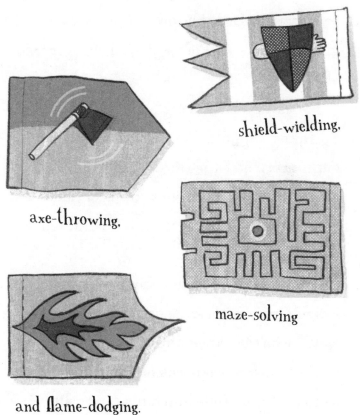

axe-throwing,

shield-wielding,

maze-solving

and flame-dodging.

3

Grace Wonder couldn't wait to get stuck in.

'Can you believe we're actually going?' Grace said to her sister, Princess Portia. 'It's so cool that everyone's invited!'

'I thought Dad would *never* agree to let girls join in,' said Portia. 'Let alone everyone else as well.'

Portia was busy tying her sleeping bag to Sprinkles's saddle. Her beautifully turned-out unicorn stood perfectly still while she tightened the buckles and straps. 'I hope we get enough time to try all the different challenges,' she said.

'*I* hope we have enough time to do them *twice*,' Grace said. 'Although if Poop gets his way, I won't be doing any at all ...'

Her bad-tempered unicorn was in no mood to go camping. He refused to stand still, bucked off the pillow she'd managed to tie to his saddle, then deliberately trod on her foot.

Grace wasn't bothered. She knew just how to get him to behave. 'I do hope Poop stays here all weekend,' she said, deliberately ignoring him. 'It will really annoy me if he comes along.'

Poop's ears pricked and a mischievous look lit up his face. He picked up Grace's backpack in his teeth and stomped his hoof on the cobbles, suddenly eager to get going.

Grace grinned. 'Let's try and get there early,' she said to Portia. 'I want to do my favourite quests at least three times!'

'Now, now, girls,' said Taffy Trafalgar, the girls' tutor, waddling towards them. The old troll wagged a furry finger at Grace. 'It's not about *how many* quests you undertake, it's about *how well you perform them*!'

'Quite right, Taffy,' said King Wonder, following close behind.

The girls' father was still wearing his robe and pyjamas, sipping hot chocolate from a mug emblazoned, REALM'S BEST DAD. 'Questival is always a big deal, and this year it's more important than ever,' he said, casting a proud eye over the bustling courtyard.

'The first-ever open-to-all Questival,' said Taffy, hopping excitedly from one rabbity foot to another. 'Now, every young knight, goblin and boggart can try their hand at questing!'

'With more people learning more skills, Wondermere will be stronger than ever,' the king agreed.

'Right,' said Grace absent-mindedly. In truth, she was worrying about Dennis. She couldn't wait to go camping; she only wished she didn't have to leave her baby dragon behind.

Grace had recently rescued his egg from the bottom of the castle moat. She'd taken care of him after he hatched, before returning him to the safety of his parents' nest. Since then, Dennis had visited Grace every day. They'd formed an unbreakable bond.

Grace's imp friend, Bram Bramwell, was in the moat with Dennis right now, playing fetch with the cheeky little dragon. Bram had turned himself into an oversized rubber duck for the occasion, the better to cope with Dennis's enthusiastic splashing.

'I hope he'll be all right,' Grace said quietly.

'Which one?' Taffy chuckled. 'The dragon or the duck?'

'They'll *both* be fine,' said Portia firmly, giving her sister a quick hug. 'We're only away for two nights. Besides, they're *both* having a great time.'

The imp waved a rubber wing at the girls and smiled broadly, before – **CLAP!** – turning himself into a canoe.

'Bram and Dennis will be just dandy,' said King Wonder. 'But who'll look after *you*? It feels like only yesterday you were tiny tots. Climbing the turrets, sliding down bannisters, swinging from the chandeliers ...'

'We *did* do all of that yesterday,' Grace laughed. Her father's eyebrows shot up in concern.

'I could always go with them, sire?' Taffy suggested. 'I daresay Ross Rigglebottom and his team of trolls could use some extra help supervising the young campers ...'

'Thanks, Taffy, but we can look after ourselves,' Portia said quickly.

'You've said it yourself, Dad,' Grace added, 'we're two of your most capable knights.'

The king looked uncertain. 'Have you both packed plenty of clean Under-Wonders?'

'Of course,' Grace said. 'You really don't need to worry. Besides, Portia's read every book about Questival ever written.'

'I've packed them all, too,' said Portia, patting a bulging bag strapped to Sprinkles's back.

'And you've remembered your best mallets?' their father asked.

'Grace was top goal scorer in the troll-o league this season,' Portia said. 'Do you honestly think she'd forget to pack her mallet?'

'I even packed a spare,' Grace said proudly. 'I'm aiming for top marks in the mallet-swinging quest!'

'Questival's not all fun and games, you know,' said Taffy, peering at her over the top of his little round glasses. 'It's an important part of Wondermerian culture!'

'There will be young people at Questival who don't know how knights ought to conduct themselves,' the king said. 'I'm relying on you two to set a good example.'

'We will,' Portia said, holding her hand to her chest. 'Knight's honour.'

'We'll be *awesome* at Questival,' Grace agreed. 'I *really* want to win the Golden Plume!'

'Ah, the Golden Plume,' King Wonder said wistfully. 'I wish *I'd* managed to win it when *I* went. I was desperate to be the best performing knight, but I just couldn't get the hang of bog-snorkelling.'

'Your father might still be in that bog if Sir Gregory hadn't pulled him out,' said Taffy seriously.

'I could've done it myself, given half a chance,' said King Wonder, blushing.

Grace frowned. 'Who's *Sir Gregory*?'

'Alas, that remains a mystery,' sighed the king. 'No one knew anything about him before he appeared at Questival and wowed everybody – and no one's seen him since.'

'No one even knows what he looks like,' said Taffy. 'He never once removed his helmet. But he was a magnificent competitor.'

'Which just proves that absolutely *anything* can happen,' said the king briskly. 'The winner could surprise us all. Knights need all sorts of qualities to triumph ...'

Grace wasn't sure about that. No one else stood a chance! She was sure to ace Questival, proving once and for all that she was more than just a girl and a princess – and an adopted one at that. She was also the realm's best knight.

She sighed happily as she pictured herself riding home to Wondermere Castle, the Golden Plume proudly fluttering on top

of her helmet, and Poop nibbling her
trousers ...

'Nibbling my trousers?! Wait, what ... ?'
Grace's daydream evaporated as Poop sank
his teeth into her bottom.

'**OUCH,** Poop!' she said, pushing his nose
away. He gave a sulky snort and stuck out
his lower lip.

'Cheer up, you big grump,' Grace said,
heaving herself into the saddle. 'As soon as
we're there, I'll give you a whole bag of
roasted hazel gums.'

That did it. At the mention of his favourite
treat, Poop broke into a trot. Portia followed
on Sprinkles, with King Wonder and Taffy
jogging alongside to keep up.

'You're sure you know the way?' the king
asked, slopping hot chocolate from his mug.

'Through the forest, just beyond the market,' Portia said.

'Relax, Dad,' Grace said, rolling her eyes. 'We've checked the map a hundred times.'

'I can't wait to get to Pixie Pastures,' said Portia happily. 'It'll be great to see so many pixies on their home turf!'

'It's very good of them to welcome so many extra campers this year,' said Taffy, bouncing along. 'Be sure to treat their home with respect!'

'We will,' Grace promised. 'So long, Taffy! Bye, Dad! See you in a few days!'

'Good luck, girls,' said Taffy, waving as they passed through the castle gates. 'May your heads be blessed with the dung of a thousand dragons!'

'A thousand and *one*,' King Wonder called

after them, wiping a tear from his eye.

Grace couldn't keep the smile from her face. She was *actually going to Questival*!

'Giddy-up, Poop,' she said as they trotted into the forest. 'We have a Golden Plume to win!'

2

DO NOT DOUBT
THE PIXIES

Telling Poop to giddy-up had been a BIG
mistake. Naturally he did the opposite,
trying his very best to make Grace late.

He stopped to graze on candy-wort at
every opportunity and insisted on having a
lengthy staring contest with each fairy they
encountered. Then, when they reached the
Forest Market, he insisted on turning around

and completing the final leg of the journey backwards.

Despite his best efforts, Grace and Portia still managed to arrive at Pixie Pastures in good time.

'I can't wait to see who else is here,' Grace said cheerfully. 'I want to check out my competition!'

As promised, she hung a bag full of roasted hazel gums over Poop's bridle. He began chewing noisily. 'Please don't pick out a good spot for our tent while you're eating,' she said, giving Portia a wink.

Poop's ears stiffened and a wicked glint came into his eyes. Still chewing, he began picking his way between the other tents, searching for a clear patch.

Grace walked beside him, taking in the

scene. Everywhere she looked was a lush carpet of bouncy green grass and beautiful wild flowers, dotted with colourful tents.

The tents came in all shapes and sizes. Some looked even older than the one the girls' father had loaned them, and very few stood perfectly upright. Most were wonky and some were still wobbling as the young campers got to grips with ropes, poles and pegs.

Those knights who had already set up camp sat around chatting, building campfires and polishing their armour. A few others were busy checking out the questing arenas clustered in the centre of the site.

'I can see troll-o goals!' said Grace, walking on her tiptoes. 'There are archery targets and climbing turrets ...'

'There's a pretty awesome-looking catapult too,' Portia added excitedly. 'Ooh, is that an assault course?!'

A trumpet gave a short, loud blast and a troll's voice rang out across the meadow. 'All knights should finish making camp. The questing arenas will open in one hour!'

Portia squealed with excitement.

'Let's hurry and put up the tent,' Grace said, following Poop towards a promising-looking clearing. 'Don't get a move on, Poop!'

'I still haven't seen a single pixie, you know,' said Portia. 'You'd think they'd be easy to spot, seeing as this is their home.'

'I'm sure we'll spot a few once questing starts,' said Grace. 'They're massive Questival fans, right?'

'Speaking of massive fans,' Portia said

quietly. 'I think a few of *yours* just spotted *you* …'

Grace took a sneaky look over her shoulder. The other campers were all whispering to one another. Now one of them stood up and pointed. 'It's Grace Wonder, Champion of Troll-o!' the girl exclaimed.

There were gasps and a loud **'OUCH!'** as another camper lost concentration and hammered his thumb instead of a tent peg.

'She's with Poop, her trusty steed,' a boy said, reaching out to pat him. Poop snorted heavily, spraying unicorn bogey in his face.

'I'm afraid he's not as trusty as you'd think,' Grace said apologetically.

The boy didn't seem to care. 'I got snotted on by Poop Wonder!' he boasted.

A wide-eyed young banshee ran over to

greet Grace. 'Is it true you hold the Wondermerian record for the longest distance a troll was ever whacked?' she asked.

'It is,' Grace said proudly. 'Twelve moat lengths, to be precise.'

The banshee squealed and handed over a quill. 'Would you please sign my helmet?! Write, *To* Sir *Lila*. I'm not a knight yet, but I want to be one, just like you.'

'Questival's a great place to start,' Grace said, scribbling a quick message.

Another camper hurried over, offering her his mallet. 'Whack me on the bottom?'

'No, whack ME on the bottom!' said another, elbowing him out of the way.

Grace turned to Portia, smiling. 'This is *wild*,' she said, but her words were drowned out by a loud buzzing sound.

'PIXIES!' cried Portia. She flung her arms wide in delight as the residents of Pixie Pastures flocked around them.

They swarmed towards Grace, jostling to get a close look at her. One settled on her helmet, two took a seat on her shoulders and several more took a perch on Poop's broad, brown bottom. They began chanting. 'Ace-y! Grace-y! Ace-y! Grace-y!'

'How *exciting*,' Portia said. 'It looks like you're the Pixies' Pick!'

'Eh?' said Grace, going cross-eyed as a pixie hovered right in front of her face.

'Whoever they make the most fuss over is likely to win the Golden Plume,' Portia explained.

'I never dreamed I'd get such a brilliant, close-up view of them.'

She tugged parchment, ink and a quill from Sprinkles's saddlebag and began making a quick sketch. 'I wish I could capture the way their wings shimmer,' she said, the tip of her tongue poking out in concentration. 'They have such cute little faces!'

'They *are* kind of cute,' Grace said, holding out her hand for a pixie to perch on.

'*Best in quest!*' it trilled.

'Thanks, little buddy,' she said. 'But my sister's got a good chance of winning the Golden Plume, too.'

The pixie turned its springy blue antennae towards Portia, then buzzed over to take a better look. 'Very good knight, but not quite right!' it announced, before flying back to Grace.

'Let us through,' a voice cried from among the growing crowd of campers. 'Kindly clear the way!' The girls' old friends, Sir Oliver and Sir Arthur, were making a path through the curious mob.

'Looks like they're keen to be seen with the Pixies' Pick,' Portia said.

'Hi, you two,' Grace said.

The boys gave the princesses a brief bow

in greeting, then turned back to address the crowd.

'This year's Pixies' Pick is a very good friend of ours,' Sir Oliver bragged.

'Did you know Sir Grace Wonder is the luckiest girl in the realm?' said Sir Arthur. ''Tis true! She's always getting covered in glorious luck muck.'

Sir Oliver gazed skyward. 'Perfect timing!' he announced. 'Watch this, everyone!'

Sure enough, a shadow fell over Grace's face as a dragon flew lazily overhead.

SPLAT!

'Oh, for bog's sake!' Grace groaned, wiping dung from her eyes.

'Behold her glittering, doo-doo-soaked splendour!' declared Sir Oliver.

The campers gasped and applauded.

'Poor pixies,' said Portia. 'Some of them got splatted, too!'

'Sorry, pixies,' Grace sighed. 'You might not want to fly so close to me.'

But the pixies didn't appear to mind. In fact, they gathered tightly around her and began singing even more enthusiastically. 'The Golden Plume's already been won! The *bestest* knight is covered in dung!'

Grace wasn't usually fond of being covered in poo, but on this occasion she was feeling pretty good about it. She was *bound* to win the Golden Plume! Luck and approximately one hundred *very enthusiastic* pixies were on her side. Nothing could stand in her way ...

Or could it? The ground began to rumble, setting all the tents a-quiver.

'Quaky shaky!' squeaked the pixie on her

helmet. The others joined in, clinging tightly to Grace and Poop. **'QUAAAAAKY SHAAAAAKY!'** they chanted in unison.

'Earthquake!' squealed Sir Arthur, diving for cover.

'What in all Wonder's happening?!' asked Portia.

Grace had no idea, but whatever it was, it was **BIG.**

3

DO NOT USE YOUR MALLET AS A HAMMER

Everyone shrieked and fretted as the ground beneath them started to tremble, but Grace stood strong. She felt sure the shaking was too rhythmical to be an earthquake – a slow and steady

BOOM,

BOOM,

BOOM!

Sure enough, the *real* cause soon made itself known.

Grace gasped as Questival's newest arrival came into view. A young giant was striding into camp. One by one, the knights stepped aside, craning their necks to get a proper look.

Grace had never expected to see a giant at Questival – giants were usually so shy.

This one looked anything *but*. She towered over the tents, nose pointing loftily in the air as she strode on by, hands on hips, not even stopping to say hello.

'Wowser!' gasped Sir Arthur, looking awestruck. 'Is that THE *Mondo Colossa*?!'

'Mondo who?' said Grace, frowning.

'Mondo's the daughter of Chief Colossa, leader of the giants,' Sir Arthur explained, gazing adoringly after Mondo as she thudded past. 'They say she's quite the all-rounder.'

'No wonder they're so proud of her in Giant Country,' said Sir Oliver. 'Just look at her! They say she's set to follow in her mother's huge footsteps.'

'I think Dad mentioned something about that in one of his bedtime lectures,' Portia said.

'Rings a bell,' said Grace thoughtfully. 'I always fall asleep before he gets to the end.'

'Mondo's amazing,' said Sir Arthur.

The pixies clearly agreed. 'Mondo is our chosen hero!' they sang,

 fluttering their wings a little faster. 'Grace's chances are now zero!'

The pixies flocked
after Mondo, leaving
Grace's side even more
quickly than they'd
arrived. Grace hoped
she didn't look as
disappointed as she felt.

'Excuse us, m'ladies,'
said Sir Oliver, bowing
hurriedly before
rushing off with Sir
Arthur and the
rest of the
crowd.

Grace
tutted. 'So
much for
loyalty!'

'I wouldn't take it personally,' Portia said, putting away her quill. 'Everyone's just so excited to be at Questival, meeting new people. They'll calm down once the questing starts.'

'If Mondo's such a big deal, what's she doing here anyway?' Grace asked grumpily. 'Doesn't she have more important things to do back in Giant Country?'

Portia shrugged. 'Questival's open to *all*. Cheer up! The more competition, the better. Right?'

'I s'pose,' Grace grumbled.

'Anyone the pixies make a fuss of is bound to be good,' Portia said. 'I'm looking forward to meeting her. It looks like Poop is too!'

Grace had been so busy brooding over the pixies' sudden change of heart, she hadn't noticed that Poop had sneaked away. He was trotting excitedly after Mondo with the rest of her adoring fans.

'Don't come back, Poop!' she yelled, expecting him to return disobediently to her side.

But Poop didn't even bother turning round. He was too busy trying to stick his nose into Mondo's enormous backpack.

'Traitor!' Grace cried, clenching her hands into fists.

'He's probably just after a *giant* snack,' Portia said. 'Let's go introduce ourselves to Mondo – and stop him eating all of her supplies.'

'Fine,' Grace huffed, following her sister through the crowd. 'But we can't stand around chatting all day; we still have a tent to put up.'

The girls squeezed their way past their fellow campers. A young knight nudged Grace. 'Isn't Mondo amazing?'

'If you say so,' Grace muttered.

The giant was standing in a clearing, nose still aloft. She dropped her backpack casually to the ground with a **THUD**.

'PERFICK,' she boomed, planting her hands firmly on her hips. 'THIS WILL DO.'

The crowd *oohed* and *aahed* as Mondo pulled an enormous troll-o mallet out of her backpack and began using it to hammer in tent pegs.

SWISH, BANG!

SWISH, BANG!

SWISH, BANG!

'Now *that's* an impressive swing,' said Sir Oliver dreamily. 'I bet she'd be incredible at troll-o.'

'Hrmph,' said Grace.

Meanwhile, Poop stuck his nose deeper into the giant's unguarded luggage. He pulled out a paper bag filled with the largest hazel gums Grace had ever seen and began greedily gobbling them down.

'Chew properly,' she scolded. 'We don't want you getting gassy.'

On cue, Poop lifted his scruffy tail. The air filled briefly with the scent of roses, before giving way to rotten egg. Poop gave a satisfied snort, then ambled off to join Sprinkles, who was grazing in a nearby grove of marshmallow saplings with the other unicorns.

'**POOH!**' Mondo said, peering down her nose at Grace. 'WAS THAT *YOU?*'

'*Me?!*' said Grace, furiously. 'How dare you!'

'It was my sister's unicorn,' Portia said quickly. 'We're Portia and Grace Wonder, it's good to meet you.'

But Mondo ignored her and turned away again, nose in the air as she carried on hammering in pegs.

Grace raised her eyebrows. 'Rude!'

Portia shrugged. 'Maybe she didn't hear us? She has, like, ten pixies singing right in her ears.'

'Mondo is so big and clever,' the pixies crooned. 'She's the very best knight ever!'

'*Best knight?*' Grace huffed, tugging Portia away from the crowd. 'What kind of knight uses their troll-o mallet to bang in tent pegs?!'

Portia shrugged. 'She seems like she knows what she's doing ...'

Grace sneaked a glance back over her shoulder. Mondo stood, wide-legged, swinging her mallet easily with one arm while the other hand still rested on her hip. She looked super confident. Grace only wished *she* felt the same way. Maybe Mondo really *was* the better knight?

She certainly seems to think *she's better than everyone*, Grace thought to herself as they slunk away from the crowd.

'Her tent must be massive,' she said at last. 'Come on. Let's go bag a camping spot before she takes up all the room.'

4

DO NOT COUNT YOUR DRAGONS BEFORE THEY HATCH

'We could put the tent *here*?' Portia suggested, marching towards a clear patch of grass. 'It's nice and flat, plus it's not too far from the questing arenas.'

'Whatever,' Grace said sulkily.

In all honesty she wasn't paying attention. She couldn't stop imagining her father handing Mondo the Golden Plume at

Questival's closing ceremony …

'Welcome, princesses!'

Her unpleasant daydream ended abruptly as a troll wearing a *Questival Leader* bib waddled over to greet them. He had a large, twirly moustache and was carrying a clipboard. He bowed so deeply his ears draped along the ground.

'It's an honour to welcome you to Questival. Ross Rigglebottom, at your service.'

'Nice to meet you, Mr Rigglebottom,' said Portia, curtsying.

Grace gave him a half-hearted bow and a gruff, 'Hullo.'

'I'm rather surprised to see the pair of you aren't surrounded by pixies,' said the troll, tucking his clipboard under his arm. 'I'd assumed you'd be mobbed, top-scoring young troll-o stars that you are!'

'There's no danger of that,' Grace said sulkily. 'They're all hanging around Mondo Colossa.'

'Mondo Colossa is here?!' Ross squeaked. 'Goodness! If I'd known we were expecting a giant, I'd have made the washroom tent bigger!'

'Mondo seems to be this year's Pixies' Pick,' Portia said.

'Although they'd picked *me* out before she arrived,' Grace added grouchily.

Ross shook his head. 'Don't count your dragons before they hatch!

Questival's winner is never a foregone conclusion, no matter *what* the pixies say.'

Grace stood up tall and straightened her helmet. 'Is that really true?'

'Absolutely,' Ross said. 'The pixies are certainly a good yardstick, but they don't always get it right. There's more to Questival than meets the eye – just ask your father!'

'Oh, he's told us,' said Portia, pushing her glasses up her nose. 'We know all about Sir Gregory.'

Ross chuckled. '*No one* knows all about Sir Gregory, not even the pixies. Questival was designed to challenge the very best of knights. The strongest may fail, the weakest may triumph,' Ross continued. 'The stakes change with every quest you undertake. Sometimes handling new friendships can be the toughest challenge of all.'

'I can't wait to get started!' Grace said happily.

'Glad to hear it,' said Ross. 'Now, would you like a quick rundown of the rules?'

'Yes, please,' said Portia.

The troll cleared his throat. 'The questing begins at noon today. Fit in as many quests as you're able before first starlight, when the arenas will close.'

'They *close*?' Grace said, disappointed.

'They reopen at sunrise,' Ross assured her. 'But trust me, after setting up camp and spending a full afternoon questing, you'll be more than ready for bed. Be sure to get a good night's rest, because tomorrow you'll be questing *all day*.'

'Yessss!' said Grace, punching the air.

'If you miss a quest, or you want to repeat any to improve your score, you'll have a little time to try on the final day, before King Wonder arrives to award the Golden Plume to our top-scoring knight.'

Which will be ME, Grace thought to herself. *No matter what the pixies think.*

5

DO NOT BE A BIG, SNOOTY SHOW-OFF

The girls were pleasantly surprised to discover that, ancient though it was, their father's tent was the pop-up kind. As they unrolled it, it sprang into shape – **FFFLAM!** – sending out a cloud of dust and glitter.

Grace crawled inside. 'Bagsy I sleep *this* side; the other side pongs.'

Portia crawled in after her, wrinkling

her nose. 'Ugh! Where's that awful smell coming from?'

'There's something small and spotty curled up in the corner,' Grace said, pointing.

'Ooh, maybe it's a hibernating hobgoblin?' said Portia, reaching out to grab it. A horrified look came over her face. **'EEW!** It's one of Dad's old socks!'

'Evacuate!' cried Grace, flinging open the tent flaps and crawling quickly outdoors.

Portia clambered after her, holding the sock at arm's length in one hand and pinching her nose with the other. 'We could give it to Verity to use in one of her revolting potions?' she suggested. 'We'll be passing the market again on the way home ...'

'Or we could burn it on the campfire later?' Grace suggested.

'No way,' said Portia. 'It might taint our toast.'

In the end, the girls settled for tying the sock to the top of their tent. 'I guess it'll make our tent easy to spot from the arenas,' Grace said.

'Home sweet home,' said Portia, watching it flutter gently in the breeze.

'We finished in the nick of time,' Grace said, dusting off her hands. 'Let's get questing!'

The girls linked arms and joined the stream of campers heading towards the arenas. Grace felt more settled now they'd made camp. She was sure she would win the pixies back around with a solid performance that afternoon.

She glanced over at Mondo as they passed the giant's camping pitch. She was still struggling to put up her enormous tent – a huge, round, striped one that reminded Grace of the big top she'd seen when the Gloranian Travelling Circus visited Wondermere.

'Maybe we should lend her a hand?' Portia suggested. 'It can't be easy with all those pixies buzzing around.'

'If Mondo's really all *that* amazing she ought to be able to figure out a few tent poles by herself,' said Grace.

It felt good to see her main competitor struggling, but all the same, Grace knew she was being a little unkind. She quickly changed the subject. 'Which quest shall we do first?'

To their left was the target practice arena: a ringed enclosure containing a rack of bows and arrows and a row of round boards painted to look like ogres' bottoms. To their right stood another arena, containing the highest troll-o goalpost Grace had ever seen.

Portia shouldered her mallet. 'Mallet-swinging, then target practice,' she said firmly. 'Then *please* can we do pin-the-tail-on-the-stick-man? I've never seen a real life stick creature before, let alone had the chance to give one a tail.'

'Sure,' Grace agreed. She gave her mallet a practice swing, flipped down her helmet's visor and led the way into the arena. 'Let's show everyone how it's done.'

Grace went first, swinging her mallet in an elegant arc and sending the volunteer ball-troll soaring.

'YAHOOOOEY!'

he cried happily, flying
through the goal.

Portia applauded, along with
the other competitors lined up to take
part. Grace took off her helmet and bowed.

'Top marks, Sir Grace!' said Ross
Rigglebottom, waddling over and making a
note on his clipboard. 'That was quite the
masterclass. I'm sure our campers who are
new to questing would appreciate a few tips?'

'Ooh, yes, please!' said an imp in a cardboard helmet. 'What's your number one tip for knighthood? And how do you plan to beat Mondo Colossa to the Golden Plume?'

'Oh, I'll beat her *easily*,' Grace said, giving Mondo's tent a sideways glance.

The enormous structure was finally standing, but there was no sign of the giant or her pixie cheer squad. Grace turned back to address her own fans. 'As for my top tip, that's easy: **DO NOT be a big, snooty show-off like Mondo.**'

Grace paused. Was something wrong with Portia? Her sister was waving her arms around wildly, flapping them like the wings of a particularly dizzy dragon. Perhaps she was swatting at a pixie? Whatever. Grace carried on.

'Mondo thinks she's better than everyone else, just because she's bigger ...'

A voice boomed out behind Grace, making her jump. **'GIVING OUT ADVICE, ARE WE?'**

Grace turned round and came face-to-belly with Mondo Colossa. The giant towered over her, nose aloft. 'MAYBE YOU HAVE A LICKLE ADVICE FOR ME?'

Grace gulped. 'Well, my first tip would be to stop shouting.'

'CAN'T HELP IT,' Mondo said, just as loudly. 'I GUESS SOME OF US WERE **BORN TO BOOM!'**

She made cannons with her fingers, pretended to blow smoke from their tips, then took a bow. The pixies cheered and the other knights applauded, but Grace just rolled her eyes.

'If you can't keep quiet, my *second* tip is to hurry up and get questing. If you pick up knightly skills as slowly as you put up a tent, you'll never be able to squeeze in all the challenges. Mallet-swinging isn't as easy as *I* make it look.'

'WE'LL SEE ABOUT THAT,' said Mondo, striding past Grace into the arena. The pixies followed, poking their tongues out at Grace as they went.

'Mondo never snoozes!' they chanted. 'Grace-y always loses!'

Grace stuck out her own tongue in response. 'Just watch,' she said to Portia. 'They'll come flocking back to me any minute when Mondo messes up. She'll never beat *my* score.'

6

DO NOT BE
A BAD SPORT

Mondo hadn't even picked up her mallet, but
she was already drawing quite a crowd.

More and more knights had hurried over
to spectate, joined by several of the camp
leader trolls. Even Ross Rigglebottom
lowered his clipboard to watch.

'She can't possibly score a better goal than
mine,' Grace said confidently.

'Yours was great,' Portia agreed. 'Still, I'm keen to watch Mondo in action. If she's half as good as the pixies seem to think, this could be *spectacular.*'

'No one's *that* good,' Grace scoffed.

'We love you, Mondo!' called a young knight. Mondo paid no attention, but Grace couldn't help notice it was Lila, the banshee whose helmet she'd signed. Her autograph had been crossed out. Mondo's name was scrawled beside it in big, untidy letters.

Grace tutted loudly. 'She just *loves* the attention. Did you ever meet such a loud-mouthed show-off?!'

Portia shrugged. 'You have to admit, she *is* kind of cool.'

The girls held their breath as Mondo swung back her enormous mallet and

took aim. But, wait – what in all Wonder
was she doing with her *other* hand? Grace
frowned. Could the giant *really* be stringing
a bow?

THWHACK!
TWANG!
'YEEK!'

It happened so
fast it was hard
to take it all in.
With one hand,
Mondo swung
her mallet,
sending the
ball-troll flying
delightedly
through the goal.

At the same time, she fired a bow with the other, releasing not one but *three* arrows, *all at once.*

While each arrow **THWEEENKED** neatly into the target, the giant dropped her bow, then deftly pinned a tail on a stick man, despite him being hidden among a huge pile of actual sticks.

'B-but how's that even *possible*?!' Grace spluttered.

'Amazing,' Portia breathed. 'I would *never* have spotted him, let alone so quickly.'

'**NAILED IT!**' cried Mondo, dancing gleefully around with the stick man. 'Aren't you a teensy-weensy cutiekins?!'

Grace scoffed. 'So much for calm and cool ...'

'I MEAN, WHATEVER, TWIGGY,' Mondo said, releasing the stick man back into his woodpile. She placed her hands on her hips and pointed her nose in the air. 'I WIN. *THAT'S* HOW A REAL KNIGHT DOES IT.'

Everyone cheered. The pixies were in raptures, high-fiving one another and turning cartwheels in mid-air. 'Bow and stick man! Goal and ball! Mondo is the best of all!'

'The pixies are giving Mondo an unfair advantage,' Grace grumbled. '*Anyone* would do better with a whole crowd supporting them. Besides, I expect being so tall makes everything much easier.'

'Don't be a bad sport,' Portia said, giving Grace's arm a squeeze. 'You're still *my* favourite knight. Anyhow, Mondo's size might actually be a *dis*advantage in the next quest ...'

Mondo was already striding over to the next arena.

Grace read the sign aloud. '*Welly-wanging?*' she said, frowning. 'What even *is* that?'

'You fling your boot off your foot and see how far it goes,' Portia explained.

'Mondo's *bound* to mess *this one* up,' Grace said, hurrying over to get a good viewing spot. 'Her wellies are MASSIVE, I bet they're really heavy and hard to fling.'

x

But if the giant found the challenge daunting, she didn't show it. Grace watched as Mondo strode into position. She drew back one foot, then KICKED with all her might – all the while casually studying the fingernails on her left hand, and not even *slightly* losing her balance.

FFFWEEEEEEEEEE!

Her welly went *flying*. It cleared the tent tops, sailing right over the marshmallow trees where the unicorns were grazing. Even Poop briefly stopped snacking to watch it hurtle by.

Everyone cheered – apart from Grace and the unhappy troll whose job it was to retrieve the freshly flung boots.

'At least this one'll be easy to spot,' he sighed, trudging off to fetch it.

Meanwhile, the pixies' singing was louder than ever. 'Mondo has the winning boot! Mondo has a golden foot!'

'That's so stupid,' Grace grizzled. '*Boot* doesn't rhyme with *foot*!'

'It does the way *they're* singing it,' Portia pointed out. 'Maybe we should congratulate Mondo, like everyone else? I mean, I know we want to *beat her* and everything, but you know what Dad always says. *A good knight …*'

'*… always knows another*,' Grace sighed.

She trudged over to Mondo, who was leaning one-legged against a tree, while waiting for her boot to be returned. The

pixies had buzzed off to help the troll
carry it.

'Nicely done,' Grace said grudgingly.
'You can show off about it, if you like. I
could hardly blame you.'

But Mondo beamed down at her. 'I'm *so*
happy to meet you,' Mondo said, smiling.
'You're my favourite troll-o star. I have an
enormous poster of you on my wall.'

'Riiiiight ... well, don't let us keep you
from your winning streak,' said Grace,
hurriedly tugging her sister away.

'What's wrong with you?' Portia asked.
'She was being really nice!'

'What's wrong with *me*?!' Grace said,

astonished. 'What's wrong with *her*, more like? Who does she think she's kidding?!'

'I thought she was being really friendly ...' Portia began.

'She doesn't *normally* act that way. Not when everyone else is around,' Grace hissed. 'No *way* does she have my poster on her wall. She's just trying to lull us into a false sense of security before she tops our scores and humiliates us in front of everyone!'

'Well, she certainly won't beat *you*,' Portia said firmly. 'I reckon you can wang your welly MILES.'

'You're right,' Grace said, standing a little straighter. 'I'll soon show those pixies who's best. And why just wang my *own* welly? I'll make this challenge even harder and still come out on top.'

'What do you mean?' Portia asked, but Grace didn't answer. She was striding over to the *wanging* spot, where the boot-retrieval troll was staggering back with Mondo's boot, surrounded by a cloud of happy pixies.

'Mondo has the winning score,' they trilled. 'No point trying any more!'

'We'll soon see about that,' said Grace, taking the gigantic boot from the troll.

Mondo's boot really *was* heavy. She staggered slightly under its weight, set it on the ground and slipped her foot into it. 'Stand back, everyone,' she announced confidently. 'This boot is heading for the clouds!'

7

NEVER WANG A GIANT WELLY

Grace took a deep breath and tried to imagine herself on the troll-o pitch. That was her happy place. She knew exactly what to do without even having to think about it – and she always had a crowd to cheer her on …

'Grace can't fling this massive shoe!' the pixies taunted. 'Down with Grace-y! Boo! Boo! Boo!'

The whole campsite was watching, but most of them were cheering for Mondo. Grace perked up a little when she spotted Sir Arthur and Sir Oliver hurrying over, freshly covered in custard from the food-fighting arena.

'This is so exciting!' said Sir Oliver, taking a stand beside Portia.

'Grace will smash this,' Sir Arthur said loyally. 'She's the luckiest girl in the realm.'

'Then again,' Sir Oliver added quietly, 'Mondo *is* the Pixies' Pick ...'

Grace tried turning her focus to the task in hand. If she'd learned anything on the troll-o pitch, it was to ignore any doubts.

But this wasn't troll-o, and Mondo's boot was a lot heavier than it looked ...

The crowd was still growing. Even the

unicorns had stopped eating and strolled over to watch. Grace had never been so pleased to see Poop.

'I should've known *you'd* have my back,' she said, giving his rump a pat.

But Poop gave a dismissive snort and trampled on by, sticking his nose into Mondo's oversized pocket. 'NAUGHTY PONY!' the giant giggled.

'Poop's *not* a pony, he's a *unicorn*,' Grace snapped. 'And a traitorous one at that.'

'Focus,' Portia urged quietly, 'you've got this.'

Grace tried, but it was hard. Other people might think she was the luckiest girl in the realm, but in truth, luck had nothing to do with all she'd achieved.

Since arriving at the castle on the orphan

cart, she'd become a princess, been knighted by the king and earned the title Champion of Troll-o. It had all taken hard work and dedication. That's exactly what winning Questival would take, too.

She'd come so far already. She couldn't afford to slip up now!

Grace wriggled her toes inside the enormous boot. A bead of sweat trickled out from under her helmet. But just as she raised her leg to kick off the boot, the pixies began flitting around her, pulling faces and singing.

'Fail the test! You're not best! You won't win a single quest!' One of them shoved its tiny blue bum cheeks in her face.

'Gah!' Grace cried, stumbling as she swung her foot. 'Oh, no!'

Instead of sending the boot flying *forward*,

Grace sent it straight *up*. It turned a
ponderous half-cartwheel in mid-air before
landing – **PLOOONK!** – right over her head.

The pixies cackled
in triumph.
The crowd
groaned,
some
muttering
embarrassed
commiserations as
they headed off to focus
on quests of their own.

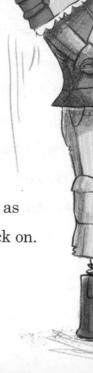

'That was rotten luck,'
said Portia, helping Grace
tug the boot off her head.

Tears stung Grace's eyes as
she pulled her own boot back on.

Mondo was the only other knight still in the arena. She strode over to retrieve her boot. To Grace's surprise, she ducked down so the pixies couldn't hear her, and whispered in Grace's ear. '*Maybe try again with your teeny-weeny boot? Mine are HUMONGOUS.*'

'Oh, stop showing off,' Grace snapped. Poop was still busily nosing around in Mondo's pockets. 'And stop trying to lure my unicorn away with treats! Isn't stealing my victory enough?!'

Mondo didn't react. She didn't seem to be paying Poop any attention, either. She was too busy frowning intently up at the sky.

'You're so *rude*,' Grace continued. 'You could at least look at me when I'm talking … Oh.'

She fell
silent as a
dragon flew
overhead, casting a
shadow over all three
girls.

'MOVE!' roared Mondo,
lunging at Grace. She
pushed her to safety in
the nick of time. A
flurry of freshly
dropped dragon
dung

SLOPPED over the giant's broad shoulders.

'Eww,' said Portia, looking Mondo up and down. 'That dragon must've had a *really* big lunch.'

'Bonus points to Mondo Colossa,' announced Ross Rigglebottom. 'A good knight always thinks of others before herself!'

Grace frowned. It was hard to tell beneath the glittery splatter, but Mondo looked very unhappy. Could it really be just because of the dung?

'I need to get wishy-washed, BIG TIME,' the giant said, hurrying off towards the wash tents, followed by her adoring pixies.

'Are you OK?' Portia asked Grace gently.

Grace was worried her voice might come

out wobbly, so she took a deep breath before replying. 'Mondo did that on purpose,' she said eventually. '*I'm* the luckiest girl in the realm, not her!'

Portia smiled. 'But you *hate* getting pooped on! You don't even believe it's lucky, remember?'

Grace shifted uncomfortably in her armour. What she wouldn't give to be covered in dung right now. 'Well, obviously I don't *believe it*,' she said, finding a small smile of her own.

'Good,' said Portia, linking her arm through Grace's. 'So if it's all the same with you, I'd like to carry on questing.'

'I'm not following Mondo around like everyone else,' Grace grumbled. 'I'll do whatever quest she's *not* doing.'

77

'Fine,' said Portia. 'Come on, there's a stick man round here somewhere, just waiting for us to give him a tail!'

8

DO NOT
GIVE UP

Grace made a magnificent comeback as the
day unfolded. By the time the first star
appeared in the indigo sky, she had *almost*
begun to enjoy herself. But all too soon, the
first day's questing came to an end.

She tugged off her armour and flopped
down on the springy grass outside their tent.

'What a beautiful evening,' sighed Portia,

lighting their little campfire. She took a saucepan out of her backpack and began preparing some hot chocolate.

Grace gazed up at the stars and smiled. It really *was* a beautiful evening. The whole meadow was aglow with the soft light of lamps and campfires. Even so, she would have felt far happier if her name was at the top of the leader board.

It wasn't. She'd finished the first day a single point behind Mondo Colossa.

Even now, the pixies were flying from tent to tent, singing, 'Have you seen the leader board? Grace can't score what Mondo's scored!'

Grace tugged off her armour and crawled inside the tent.

'I'll never win the Golden Plume at this rate,' she said quietly as Portia joined her. 'I may as well fly Dad's stinky old sock from the top of my helmet.'

'Now you're being silly,' said Portia, handing her a steaming mug of hot chocolate. 'You only slipped up on welly-wanging, and that was understandable. You could take the lead from Mondo any time.'

'Maybe,' Grace said.

'Besides,' Portia continued, sipping her own drink. 'I have a feeling Mondo is just as unhappy as you are.'

Grace frowned. 'How'd you figure that one out?'

'The pixies are basically throwing a party in her honour right now,' said Portia, wriggling into her sleeping bag. 'She ought to be enjoying herself, but she's in her tent, all alone.'

'Because she's so *snooty*, always walking round with her nose in the air,' Grace said. 'I bet she thinks she's too good for *Questival*!'

'*I* thought she was kind of sweet earlier, giving you that boot-flinging advice when no one was watching,' Portia said.

Grace merely **HARRUMPHED**.

'Maybe she's going to bed early because she's tired?' Portia suggested. 'She worked hard today. It can't have been easy, putting up that whopping great tent all by herself.'

'She didn't work *half* as hard as the pixies,' Grace said, keen to change the subject. 'I'm amazed they haven't lost their voices.'

'They're certainly dedicated,' Portia agreed. 'It'll be interesting to see what they do if Mondo ever messes up.'

'She'll *never* mess up, not with so much support,' Grace said, pulling on her bed socks. 'Although ... I've just had the most amazing idea!'

She picked up her lamp, casting half her face into shadow. Portia giggled. 'You look super sinister right now!'

'More like super *smart*,' Grace grinned. '*I* don't believe Mondo's the best knight. *I* think she's just buoyed up by the pixies.'

'So?' Portia said, stifling a yawn.

'*So,* when I'm on the troll-o pitch, it's the cheers of the crowd that help me succeed.'

'I suppose the pixies *could* be giving her an advantage ...' Portia said.

'And they're giving everyone else a *dis*advantage,' Grace said. 'Ross Rigglebottom was right – the pixies *are* a distraction. They're distracting everyone else from finding out who's really the best.'

She swallowed her hot chocolate in one gulp, then burped. 'If we can stop the pixies cheering her on, *everyone* could get a chance to shine.'

'Maybe,' Portia yawned, laid her head on her pillow and closed her eyes. 'But the pixies have changed their prediction once already. Who says they won't change it again?'

'Oh, they *definitely* will,' said Grace, turning down the lamp. 'They'll soon go back to predicting *me* for the win. I'm going to beat them at their own game. *Distraction!*'

9

DO NOT TRUST
A FARTING KNIGHT

Grace felt much better after a good night's
sleep and nine slices of toast. Her breakfast
was slightly blackened from the flames of the
campfire, but she didn't care. She was
beginning to taste victory.

'I let myself get my Under-Wonders in a
twist yesterday,' she admitted, passing the
toasting fork to Portia. 'I'm not bothered

about Mondo any more. Thanks to my plan, everything's going to be great.'

'Are you *sure* your plan's a good idea?' Portia asked between mouthfuls. 'I mean, I know the pixies are annoying, but distracting them seems a little unfair. After all, they do *live* here, and Questival's the highlight of their year ...'

'Their *real* highlight is picking a winner,' Grace said. 'And thanks to me, they're about to meet the ultimate champion ...'

♪ ♫ ♪

Grace began putting her plan into action the minute they started questing. She strode happily into the bog-snorkelling arena, announcing loudly, 'Did anyone else see the new knight? He looks *amazing*!'

'I just spotted him in the marshmallow glade,' Portia said, pulling on a snorkelling mask. 'Four whole legs! I bet he's really good at, um ... like ... *everything*.'

Grace gave the pixies a sideways glance. They'd quietened down, antennae quivering as they strained to eavesdrop on the girls' conversation.

'Did you see all those medals on his armour?' Grace said, pulling on a pair of flippers.

'I heard his backpack clanking, too,' said Portia, pretending not to notice as the pixies flew closer. 'It must be *full* of trophies.'

The pixies couldn't help themselves. They instantly abandoned Mondo and swarmed off in the direction of the trees.

Grace was delighted. Her plan was working! But Portia seemed concerned. 'I hope we haven't upset Mondo,' she said. 'She doesn't seem like her usual self ...'

Grace frowned. Portia had a point. Instead of standing confidently with her hands on her hips, Mondo was leaning casually against a climbing tower.

Grace stiffened as the giant caught her watching.

'Where'd the lickle pickles go?' Mondo asked quietly.

It was Grace's turn to stick her nose in the air. 'They want to see the new, super-awesome competitor,' she said smugly.

'A new knight?' said Mondo, standing up straight and peering curiously towards the trees.

'They say he's bound to win the Golden Plume,' Grace said, feeling pleased with herself.

'Surely it's too late?' Mondo said. 'Questival's already halfway through!'

'If he's as good as the pixies seem to think he is, he might just manage it,' Grace said. 'So you'd better watch out – you won't be top of the leader board much longer.'

Strangely, Mondo gave Grace a delighted smile, but it quickly faded as Sir Oliver and Sir Arthur approached, flapping loudly along in snorkelling gear.

Mondo stiffened, sticking her nose in the air and taking up her usual lofty stance.

'WELL, THE NEW KNIGHT WON'T BEAT *ME*,' she boomed. **'I'M IN IT TO WIN IT!'**

Grace found her rapid change of behaviour puzzling, but there was no time to dwell on it. Sir Arthur was busy tugging at her tunic sleeve.

'Where'd all the pixies go?' he asked.

'They've found a new knight to worship,' Portia said, gazing worriedly towards the rustling trees. 'At least, I *hope* that's what they found ...'

'This cool knight just showed up,' Grace explained, cheerfully pulling on her snorkelling mask. 'He's bound to win, so the rest of us losers might as well carry on questing ...'

She made her way happily over to the bog, expecting everyone else to follow. But they were all gazing intently towards the marshmallow glade, which was abuzz with singing pixies. 'Hairy, scary, weird knight!' they chimed. 'Something isn't quite right!'

'Behold!' gasped Sir Oliver. 'The new knight is about to emerge from the trees ...'

'He's *what*?!' Portia gulped, tugging off her snorkelling mask for a better look.

'I gave him a whole bag of hazel gums,' Grace hissed. 'He's *supposed* to stay put!'

The new knight **CLANGED** out of the bushes, shrouded in saucepans, blankets and flags. The pixies followed, peering intently at the bulky knight as he began to quiver and shake. Then the knight's rear end PARPED, filling the air with the scent of roses.

'Uh-oh,' said Portia, hurriedly pinching her nose as the smell turned distinctly eggy.

Mondo bent over and whispered in Grace's ear. 'Isn't that your ickle pony?'

'He's not my *little pony*,' Grace said through gritted teeth. 'He's my *squodgin' enormous*, useless unicorn!'

'That's not a knight!' said Sir Oliver.

''Tis Poop Wonder,' cried Sir Arthur, eyes watering. 'I'd know his gassy emissions anywhere!'

As if on cue, Poop shook off his disguise. 'Grace tried cheating with a horse,' sang the pixies. 'Mondo's still the best, of course!'

Poop gave an uninterested snort, then ambled over for a nose in Mondo's pockets.

'*Tickly* ickle pony,' Mondo giggled. 'I wish I could play with you all day instead of doing more quests!'

'Eh?' said Sir Oliver, frowning.

'Er,' said Mondo, quickly nudging Poop away and clearing her throat. 'I MEAN, NICE TRY, GRACE WONDER, BUT I AM A MAGNIFICENT LEADER, AND **NOTHING WILL DISTRACT ME FROM WINNING THE GOLDEN PLUME!**'

Grace scowled, but her expression brightened as four pixies left Mondo's side and flew in her direction. 'I *knew* you guys would see sense,' she began.

But they hadn't come to praise her. 'Naughty, naughty, Grace Wonder,' they chanted, shoving Grace into the bog with all their might. 'Take a breath, you're going under!'

SPLAT!

BOG-SNORKELLING

'Zero points!' the supervising troll announced. 'Poor entry, far too much splatter.'

Portia rushed over to give Grace a hand. To their surprise, Mondo came, too. 'Are you OK?' she said, heaving Grace easily out of the bog. 'That was a MAHOOSIVE splat,' she whispered, sounding concerned.

'I'm *fine*,' Grace scowled. She swatted Mondo's hands away, heaved herself to her feet, then stalked off to get cleaned up.

Portia tugged off her flippers and raced after her. 'Distracting the pixies was worth a try,' she said.

'I bet Mondo *loved* watching me fail,' Grace said, pulling a string of bogweed from her hair.

'She seemed genuinely worried for you just now ...' Portia began.

But Grace wasn't listening. She was busy concocting a new plan.

'No *way* is Mondo a better knight than me,' she fumed. 'The pixies are wrong – *I'm* going to win the Golden Plume. If I can't *distract* those annoying little blue pests, I'll just have to find a way of keeping them busy ...'

10

DO NOT TRASH
YOUR OWN TENT

'That ought to do it!' Grace said, standing back
to admire her handiwork.

She and Portia had completed their
morning's questing in record time. While
everyone else finished up, the girls got to
work decorating their tent. It was all part of
their latest plan to deal with Mondo's
buzzing, blue fan club.

'Thanks for helping,' Grace said. 'You're the best sister in the whole wide realm.'

'I'm not just doing it for *your* benefit,' Portia smiled. '*I* want a shot at the Golden Plume, too!'

'Maybe my last plan didn't go too well, but *this one's* GENIUS,' Grace said confidently. She'd been decorating the outside of their tent while Portia tackled the inside. 'Well, my part's done. How are you getting on?'

'Just finished,' Portia said. 'Wanna see?'

Portia held the tent flap open. Grace peeped inside and gasped. 'It's perfect!'

The whole thing was festooned with bunting. Portia had piled their remaining snacks and provisions invitingly in the middle of the floor, and the canvas walls had been plastered with pages from her journal. She'd drawn pictures of Mondo on every single one.

'My first attempts didn't go so well,' Portia admitted, pointing to a few dodgy drawings in the far corner. 'But I got better.'

'They're all brilliant,' Grace said. 'And the party snacks are inspired.'

'I even made a sort of museum area with some exclusive Mondo artefacts I found near her tent,' Portia said, a little guiltily. 'A used handkerchief, a very big spoon and a HUMONGOUS hair ribbon.'

'Great work,' Grace said eagerly. 'Come and see what I've been doing ...'

Portia crawled out of the tent, got to her feet and promptly burst out laughing. Grace had hammered several colourful signposts into the ground, emblazoned with enticing messages for the pixies.

MONDO COLOSSA APPRECIATION SOCIETY

SQUODGIN' 'NORMOUS TREATS

PIXIES WELCOME!

'Operation Pixie Paradise is ready to go,'
Grace said, wiping her hands on her tunic.

'The pixies are going to love it. Once they're all inside, we'll seal up the tent and leave them to it. They won't be bothering us for *ages*.'

'I bet they could happily stay in there forever,' Portia agreed.

'Happy pixies, happy campers,' said Grace. 'Everyone wins.'

'Can we get back to questing now?' asked Portia. 'Everyone else is still hard at it, we could squeeze in a few more before dark ...'

'Absolutely,' said Grace. 'Just as soon as we've summoned the pixies ...'

But the pixies didn't need summoning. Before Grace could even put her helmet back on, they'd zoomed right past the girls and into the tent.

THIS WAY

'I guess they read your signs,' Portia said, ducking as the last of the swarm zoomed past her.

'Quick,' Grace said. 'Shut the door!'

The girls did their best to close the canvas flaps, but the tent was shaking wildly as the pixies darted around inside it.

'It won't stay closed!' cried Portia, tugging the door as hard as she could.

'Pull it tighter!' said Grace, trying to help.

For a short while, the pixies buzzed happily around in the writhing tent. But very quickly, their excited chatter turned sour.

'Call *that* a spoon?' a squeaky voice complained.

'What a rip-off!' moaned another.

'This is BORING!' yelled several all together.

'Uh-oh,' Portia said darkly. 'They're not even bothering to rhyme!'

'So?' said Grace.

'That's a *bad sign*,' Portia said ominously. 'Pixies sing when they're *happy*. Right now, they're not happy *at all* ...'

Grace winced, still gripping the tent tightly as the pixies' complaints grew into a deafening whine. 'Watch out, I think it's going to ...'

RR–RRR–RIP!

The tent tore clean up the middle as the pixies surged back outside, each one red-faced and absolutely *furious*.

The whole mob flew angrily into Grace's face, wagging their fingers sternly.

'Grace's party was no fun! Mondo's still our favourite one! Grace's quest will be a flop! Give up, Grace! You smell like plop!'

They led the other pixies away in a thrumming, raging thundercloud, leaving Grace and Portia in disgrace – and their camp in disarray.

'Great,' Grace groaned, surveying the damage. 'Now the pixies hate me more than ever!'

'And we have nowhere to sleep,' Portia sighed, exhausted.

Ross Rigglebottom came hurrying over, looking extremely cross.

'I've received several complaints from your fellow campers,' he said, pointing at Grace with his quill. 'They say *you* are even more of a distraction than the pixies!'

'Really?' said Grace, surprised.

'At first I thought they were just jealous of your talents,' Ross tutted, 'but I see now envy has nothing to do with it. Your camp is a disgrace – and so is your behaviour!'

'I'm sorry,' Grace said truthfully.

Ross sighed. 'I'm sure you are, but a mess is still a mess – and **messes do not belong at Questival**. Clean it up at once!'

'Yes, Mr Rigglebottom,' Grace said glumly.

'So much for fitting in some more quests,' said Portia miserably as the troll waddled away. 'The day's already over!'

Grace barely had time to pick up the broken tent poles before Mondo came striding over from the boulder-smashing arena.

She shooed the pixies away, then leaned down to speak to the girls quietly. 'Is everything OK? The pixies were singing something about ruined tents and WHOPPING dents?'

'No,' Grace said honestly. 'Everything is NOT OK. Our tent's ruined and I'm slipping further and further down the leader board. I'll never win the Golden Plume at this rate, and I'll *certainly* never be the Pixies' Pick again. They can't stand me and I'm letting everyone down!'

Portia gave her sister a hug, but Grace still looked utterly miserable. 'I'm so glad Dad can't see us now,' she sniffed, doing her best not to cry. 'He'd be so disappointed.'

Mondo looked around to check no one was watching, then scooped them both into a giant hug. 'You poor lickle things,' she said. 'Why don't you stay in my tent tonight? It's GINORMOUS enough for all three of us.'

Grace's astonished mouth was just forming a very firm, '*No*,' but Portia picked up her skirts and curtsied gratefully.

'Thank you,' she said, smiling broadly. 'We'd be honoured.'

11

ALWAYS SHARE
YOUR PROBLEMS

'Come on in!' Mondo said sweetly, ushering the girls inside. She turned back to address the pixies. **'NOT *YOU*,'** she said firmly, holding up a hand to stop them coming any further. 'IT'S BEDTIME AND I NEED A BIG, BIG REST!'

The pixies buzzed away, singing, 'Mondo's spoken! Mondo's right! Sweet dreams to our favourite knight!'

Grace stepped through the enormous doorway. '*Whoa!*' she gasped, awestruck.

'Welcome to my tent,' said Mondo shyly, stooping slightly to fit inside.

Mondo's tent was HUGE. She could stand up straight anywhere inside it and still not reach the top. It was luxurious, too. The ceiling was strung with pretty twinkle lights and the walls were draped in decorative hangings. An oversized hammock was slung between two tent posts and every corner was piled with plump pillows.

'There's even a carpet,' said Portia, delighted.

'It was really kind of you to invite us in,' said Grace, giving Mondo a genuine smile. 'Especially as I haven't exactly been the

most … well, that is … it's just… er, you see…'

'My sister is extremely competitive,' Portia said, putting an arm around Grace. 'Sometimes it gets the better of her.'

Grace bit her lip. 'Sorry,' she said sincerely.

'Gosh, no problem,' Mondo said, turning a little pink. 'But you needn't worry about having any competition from *me*. I'm not bothered about winning at all.'

'Really?' Portia said. 'You always seem so focused?'

'Do I? Goody gumdrops! I was hoping it would look that way.'

'What do you mean?' Grace said.

Mondo sighed sadly. 'Mum told me I had to make a BIG impression here and behave like a leader. She was all, "*Stand tall, stick your nose in the air and your hands on hips, and* don't let anyone see how you feel on the inside …"'

'So your confidence … and your big booming voice … it was all an act?' Grace was astonished.

Mondo sighed sadly. 'I'm trying my best to act like Mum told me, but I can't stand it when the *lickle pickles* get all excited and draw everyone's attention my way.'

'Surely you're enjoying the quests?' Grace asked, perplexed. 'You seem so good at them!'

'Oh, questing's fun,' Mondo said sadly. 'I just wish I could join in without the **WHOLE WHOPPING REALM** watching.'

'You must be finding Questival really hard,' said Portia.

'Kind of,' Mondo grimaced. 'I just want to make Mum proud.'

'Is this her tent?' Grace asked, looking around. 'We're borrowing our dad's. Yours is much bigger.'

Mondo nodded. 'Mum's MUCH bigger than me. She's much more *everything* than me.' She sighed, the resulting breeze rustling the tent's canvas walls.

'How do you mean?' asked Portia, settling into a pile of pillows.

'*She's* not shy and quiet at all,' Mondo said, flopping into her hammock. 'It makes her a great leader. How will I ever follow in her footsteps? Just imagine having everyone watching to see what you'll do next … I can't think of anything worse!'

Grace chuckled. 'And *I* can't think of anything better!'

Portia smiled. 'You're certainly an

awesome competitor, Mondo. You're a very talented knight.'

'Portia's right,' Grace said. 'You're brilliant. I wish I had a crowd of pixies cheering *me* on.'

Mondo smiled. 'I expect they're just impressed by my RIDUNKULOUS size. People always are. But why does no one care that I'm a brilliant pen pal? Or that I've collected every single piece of swamp gum I've ever chewed? Surely that's more interesting than my height?'

'I keep all *my* old gum, too!' said Grace, delighted.

'I bet your *mum*'s proud of everything you do,' said Portia. 'Even the shy stuff!'

'Maybe ...' Mondo said quietly.

'I'm sorry you're not really enjoying Questival,' Grace said sheepishly. 'And I'm *extra* sorry if I've made it worse.'

'Are you KIDDING? You've made it A SQUILLION TIMES more fun,' Mondo said, grinning. 'Watching you two enjoying yourselves is so inspiring. You make leadership look fun.'

Grace sighed. 'I've been a pretty terrible leader these last couple of days. I've been so focused on winning that I haven't been a good knight at all. I didn't even notice you were feeling unhappy.'

'No one's perfect,' Mondo said. 'Not even Grace Wonder, CHAMPION OF TROLL-O ...' The giant pulled back a tapestry hanging above her hammock. **TA-DAA!**

'Wow,' said Grace, surprised and delighted to see there really *was* a poster of her and Poop fixed up above Mondo's bed. 'You weren't kidding!'

'I'm LITERALLY your biggest fan,' Mondo said shyly. 'I'm sure you'll win the Golden Plume.'

'Thanks,' said Grace. 'I really want to. I just *love* the thrill of victory! Plus I just feel like I have so much to prove to everyone, you know? That girls CAN be knights, that orphans CAN be princesses ...'

'That princesses CAN eat ice cream for breakfast,' Portia said, chuckling.

Mondo laughed too. 'I wish *I* had a sister to share everything with,' she said. 'Including the spotlight.'

Grace sat up straight. 'What if there were a way to take the spotlight *off* you?'

Mondo raised an enormous eyebrow. 'Anything that stops me standing out is a **WHOPPING WINNER** with me.'

But Portia shook her head. 'I'm not sure it's possible. The pixies aren't easily diverted; goodness knows we've tried.'

'There has to be a way,' Grace said, frowning. 'How about we disguise you as an over-achieving bush?'

'Mondo's height might give it away,' Portia said.

'A tree, then? We could cover you in leaves and marshmallows ...'

Mondo chuckled. 'Poop would probably try to eat me.'

'How about wearing a tent?' Grace suggested. 'I bet the pixies wouldn't notice if one moved around a bit.'

'She wouldn't be able to see out,' said Portia. 'Can you imagine how dangerous the axe-throwing quest would be?'

Everyone was silent for a while, lost in thought.

Then a smile spread across Grace's face. 'I've got it!' she said, leaping up and dancing across the carpet. She heaved Mondo out of the hammock and on to her feet. 'We can make it so you won't stand out at *all*!'

'Seriously?!' said Mondo, joining in the dance.

'*Seriously*,' said Grace, tugging Portia to her feet, too. 'By the time we're finished, you'll be the least noticeable knight in all the realm. Come on, you two. We've got a *real* quest to complete!'

12

DO NOT
PANIC THE PIXIES

The campsite was almost silent as the girls
tiptoed quietly into the forest.

'We'll be in so much trouble if anyone
catches us,' Portia whispered.

'They won't,' Grace said as they headed
deeper into the woods. 'Forest Market, here
we come!'

'And you're *sure* this friend of yours will

help me?' Mondo said quietly, ducking to avoid a branch. 'I mean, I never even met her.'

'Of course she'll help,' Grace said confidently. 'Verity's great.'

'Her spells have been a little unreliable in the past,' Portia added truthfully. 'But she's been practising a lot, and she's definitely getting better.'

Mondo gulped.

'You'll be fine,' Grace said, striding fearlessly along the moonlit path. 'Besides, it's worth the risk.'

'I suppose …' said Mondo doubtfully.

'The market's closer than I thought,' said Portia. 'I see the lights ahead!'

'We'll be back at Questival before anyone notices we're gone,' said Grace happily. 'And then no one will notice Mondo at *all*.'

Most of the market stalls had already closed for the night, but the Merriwinkles' cauldron was still bubbling away.

'What are you two doing out so late?' asked Verity as the girls approached. 'I thought you were meant to be camping?'

'We are,' Grace said. 'Our friend just needs a quick favour. Verity, meet Mondo Colossa!'

'She's being plagued by pixies,' Portia added. 'It's ruining her Questival.'

'Nice to meet you,' said Mondo, peeping shyly out from between the girls.

Verity shook Mondo's huge hand in her wrinkly green ones. 'Nice to meet you, too,' she said. 'But I don't see any pixies?'

'They're asleep right now,' Mondo said, blushing. 'But they're a MAHOOSIVE nuisance whenever they're awake.'

'I can well believe it,' Verity said seriously.
'Pixies get right up my schnoz!'

The young witch tapped her nose with a
crooked green finger. Her pet spider dropped
out of it on a single, delicate thread. Verity
sniffed him back up. 'So, what exactly can I
do to help?'

'We're hoping you might be able to turn me
a TEENSY bit COMPLETELY invisible?'
Mondo said.

'If the pixies can't see Mondo, we figure
they'll pipe down and leave her alone,' Portia
explained.

'She's not enjoying the attention,' Grace
said. 'But she deserves to enjoy Questival.'

'Fair enough,' Verity said, turning her face
up to meet Mondo's. 'But if we turn you
invisible, no one *else* will be able to see you,

either. Won't that make questing *pointless*? I mean, isn't Questival all about showing off your skills?'

Mondo sighed. 'That's what Mum says, too!'

Grace shook her head firmly. 'Questival's about learning new skills, having fun, working together and making new friends.'

Mondo beamed down at her. 'Sounds **MEGA!'**

'If you say so,' said Verity. 'But how will you do all that if no one knows you're there?'

'We'll make sure the other knights and trolls know Mondo's still around,' Portia explained. 'We'll just keep her a secret from the *pixies*.'

Verity shrugged. 'I guess I can brew something up, but first I need to clean my cauldron – I just finished giving a Wonderworm magic legs.'

'You gave a Wonderworm *legs*?!' Portia exclaimed.

'Twenty, to be precise,' Verity said proudly, wiping her cauldron with a sparkling rag. 'Each with a different shoe.'

'Awesome,' gasped Mondo, gazing appreciatively at Verity.

'Yes, I am,' said Verity, grabbing armfuls of bottles and jars from her shelves. 'Let's see: fairy dust, dragon scales, toad juice ...'

'Is your gran not around to help?' Grace asked, looking around hopefully for the more experienced witch.

'She's just getting ready,' Verity said. 'She has a date tonight. But don't worry, I've seen her make invisibility potions heaps of times.'

Verity dumped the ingredients into her cauldron, bottles and all, then gave it a stir with her wand. Grace watched as the mixture turned from pale pink to bright yellow with orange spots. 'Does it look like that when your gran makes it?' she asked.

'Of course,' Verity tutted. 'Invisibility potions are a doddle.'

'So long as you don't panic the pixies,' said a voice behind Grace, making her jump. She spun around, then jumped again. Coming face-to-face with Old Mother Merriwinkle was always a little alarming, especially since Verity had accidentally given her antlers. She looked even more striking in lipstick and pine-cone hair curlers.

Mondo raised a giant eyebrow. 'What do you mean, *panic*?'

'Pixies are a nervy sort,' Verity's grandmother explained, taking a deep sniff of Verity's brew. 'Not bad, needs a touch more lizard gizzards.'

Grace watched, disgusted, as Verity **SPLOPPED** something pink and blobby into the cauldron.

'Gran's right,' the young witch said, not

even looking up from her work. 'You think the pixies are bad *now*? Just wait until you see them upset. If just *one of them* gets in a tizzy, they'll *all* start to feel the same.'

'They swarm when they panic,' said Old Mother Merriwinkle, rolling a pine-cone curler into the long, wiry hair growing from her chin wart. 'Just ask your father. He was Pixies' Pick, back in the day. When Sir Gregory beat him to the Golden Plume, the pixies got in a right strop!'

'I'd love to know more about Sir Gregory,' Grace said eagerly.

'Dad barely told us anything,' said Portia. 'I guess it's still a sore point.'

'I expect he'd tell you more, if he could,' said Old Mother Merriwinkle. 'Truth is, few people know where Sir Gregory came from, and even fewer know where he went. One thing's certain, he out-quested your father, fair and square.'

'Well, no one's going to out-quest *us*,' Grace said firmly. 'We just need to keep the pixies at bay so Mondo can relax and enjoy herself.'

'As I say, just be careful,' warned the old witch. 'The slightest thing can set pixies off.'

'I don't see how making it look like Mondo's dropped out of Questival would *panic* them?' said Portia. 'Surely they'll just move on, get over it and pick someone else to cheer for?'

'Let's hope so,' Old Mother Merriwinkle said. 'Now, if you'll excuse me, I've got places to be. Don't wait up, Verity!' She straddled her broomstick, kicked off from the ground and flew off over the treetops.

'This potion's ready, if you are?' Verity said, putting down her wand. She filled a ladle with the spotty mixture and handed it to Mondo.

'Here goes ...' the giant said, drinking the mixture in one giant gulp.

'We can still see you,' said Grace, disappointed.

Verity rolled her eyes. 'Give it a chance.'

'Can you feel anything happening?' asked Portia.

'No,' said Mondo sadly, then her face lit up. 'Wait! There's an EENSY-WEENSY tingle in my tootsies ...'

'Your bootlaces are disappearing!' Grace said, pointing at Mondo's feet.

'Your boots and socks are going, too!' said Portia, jumping up and down.

Mondo gazed down at her bare feet. 'What if my Under-Wonders disappear, but the rest of me doesn't?!'

'Don't worry,' Grace said, gazing at her friend in amazement. 'The rest of you is going now, too!'

The giant was fading from view entirely. After her feet vanished, her legs quickly disappeared, followed immediately by her entire top half. Grace and Portia stared at each other in disbelief. There was nothing left to see.

'Mondo … ?' Grace said, gawping at the space where her friend ought to be. 'Are you still there?'

'You bet I am!' said Mondo, sounding absolutely delighted. 'Thanks, Verity! This is **MAHOOSIVELY** cool!'

'So, how does she change back to normal?' Portia asked.

'It'll wear off by itself,' said Verity. 'Eventually.'

Mondo – or rather, the gap that contained her – whimpered.

'*Eventually?*' said Grace. 'How long's that?'

Verity tapped her chin thoughtfully. 'It might last a month, maybe longer. This was a *giant* dose, after all.'

'But I HAVE to reappear by the end of Questival,' Mondo said. 'Mum wants me to show everyone what an amazing leader I am! Can you imagine how cross she'll be if I get back to Giant Country and she can't even SEE ME?!'

Verity rolled her eyes. 'If you want to be *boring*, I can tell you how to reverse the magic.'

'I never knew you could reverse magic,' said Grace, intrigued.

'Only certain potions,' Verity said. 'You have to wish to reverse it with all your heart, then say, "Spell be done! Kazoo! Kazam! Show me as I truly am!"'

'Got that, Mondo?' asked Grace.

'Got it,' said the gap where Mondo once stood.

'Just be careful what you wish for,' said Verity sternly. 'If you *do* choose to reverse the spell, **you'll never be the same again.**'

Mondo gulped. 'Never?!'

'Keep your great big chin up,' Verity said. 'I thought you knights were supposed to be fearless and bold?!'

'We are,' said Grace firmly. 'Right, team?'

Portia and Mondo mumbled a rather unconvincing reply.

'Thanks, Verity,' Grace said, rolling up her sleeves. 'Let's head back to camp and see if your spell fools the pixies!'

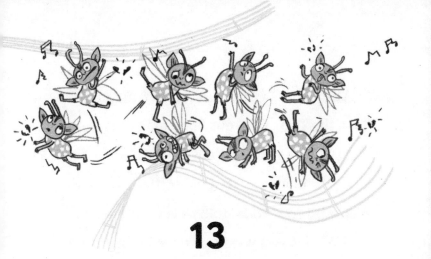

13

DO NOT INVENT
GIANT SLUGS

The sun was just beginning to rise as the
girls made their way quietly back through
the campsite.

Ross Rigglebottom was up early, discussing
the day's work with his team of supervisors.
He waved to the girls as they approached.

'Up already?' he said cheerily. 'That's the
spirit, you two.'

'Absolutely,' Grace said, breezing past. 'Just the two of us, out for a morning walk!'

As soon as the trolls were behind them, Mondo whispered, 'I'm as **WHOPPING** as ever, and the trolls didn't even notice me!'

'We'll let everyone know you're still here, just as soon as we've convinced the pixies you're gone,' Grace whispered. 'Let's go and break the bad news ...'

The pixies were still fast asleep, piled outside Mondo's tent in an untidy blue heap.

'Aww,' Portia said, bending down to take a closer look. 'They're so cute when they're sleeping.'

'Sure, they're adorable when they're *silent*,' Grace added. 'Well, here goes nothing. Are you ready, Mondo ... ?'

'You can't see, but I'm doing a double-thumbs-up,' the giant said quietly.

Grace cleared her throat and announced loudly, 'Have you heard the news? Mondo Colossa has had to leave Questival!'

Nothing.

'It's not working!' hissed Mondo.

Grace tried again. 'I hear she's gone back to Giant Country.'

An antenna wiggled.

'It's such a shame,' said Portia. 'She left before we could even say goodbye.'

A wing twitched. 'It's working!' whispered Mondo. 'Keep going!'

'Questival won't be the same without that wonderful giant,' Grace said. 'I wonder who will be champion now that Mondo's gone?'

That did it. A hundred pairs of eyes blinked open. A pixie left the top of the pile, flew right up to Grace's face and looked her straight in the eye. 'Mondo … *go go*?' it asked, its voice wobbling with anxiety.

'Yes, Mondo *go go*,' Grace told the miserable creature. 'In fact, she already *went went*. I'm afraid you just missed her.'

More and more pixies flocked closer to listen. 'Trouble in Giant Country, apparently,' Grace continued. 'She's *such* an awesome knight she simply couldn't leave her friends and family to deal with it by themselves.'

The pixies rose as one, taking to the air in a frantic blur of wings. 'Oh, no no!' they chimed, flying together in a whirling tornado. 'Mondo go go!'

Knights began poking their heads

curiously out of their tents, blinking blearily at the rising sun.

'**NO, NO! NO!**' the pixies chanted, flapping their wings frantically. 'NO MONDOOOO!'

Sir Oliver and Sir Arthur dragged themselves out of their tent and staggered over.

'What are they buzzing on about now?' asked Sir Arthur, rubbing his eyes.

Portia gave the boys an exaggerated wink. 'Mondo's had to leave.'

'Just a *teensy, teensy lickle bit of trouble* in Giant Country,' Grace said, tapping her nose.

'What?!' gasped Sir Oliver, whose hair was sticking up in wild tufts.

Grace spoke slowly and clearly so every

single pixie would hear. 'Mondo's heading home to help out with a giant emergency.'

She tapped her nose again, and even winked for good measure, but it was no use. The boys were still half asleep.

'What sort of an emergency?!' asked Sir Oliver.

'It's not a *real* emergency —' Portia said quietly, but Mondo jabbed an invisible finger in her side.

'*Shh!*' she whispered urgently. '*Not in front of the LICKLE PICKLES!*'

A nearby pixie swivelled its antennae towards Mondo. Its little blue brow furrowed as it frowned at the space between the two princesses.

'... M-Mondo?' it asked.

'Nope, definitely not,' Grace said firmly.

'*No* Mondo. She's gone. She said the emergency had something to do with, um … er … what was it again, Portia?'

'Giant … slugs?' Portia said quickly.

'*Giant slugs?!*' said Grace, giving Portia a questioning look before composing herself. 'Yes, now I come to think of it, that *was* it.'

'Yeah,' said Portia.

'They're really big and really *squishy*.'

'EEEUGGHH!' said Sir Arthur with a shiver.

'Slime everywhere, apparently,' Grace said, knowing the pixies were hanging on her every word.

'Still, not to worry. You know how capable Mondo is. I'm sure she'll have the place cleaned up in no time.'

She gave another theatrical wink, but the boys still weren't catching on. They were as distraught as the pixies.

'This is terrible,' said Sir Oliver. 'We have to *do* something!'

'We must,' agreed Sir Arthur. 'But first, we should get out of our pyjamas!'

Portia breathed a sigh of relief as the boys hurried back to their tent.

'No Mondo!' the pixies warbled.

Grace addressed them directly. 'Never mind. You'll just have to find someone else to cheer for.'

The pixies formed a tight huddle in mid-air, buzzing furiously.

'What are they doing?' asked Portia, leaning in to get a better look.

'They seem to be having some kind of meeting,' Grace said. 'I expect they're picking a new Questival champion.'

'No they're not!' said Portia. 'They're leaving!'

Grace watched, aghast, as each and every pixie flew right out of Pixie Pastures towards the distant purple mountains that marked the beginning of Giant Country.

'The lickle pickles are gone!' cried Mondo triumphantly. She lifted Grace and Portia off their feet in a giant, invisible hug. 'I can carry on questing without everyone staring at me!'

'They may not have picked a new champion,' Grace said, smiling as Mondo set her back on the ground. 'But they've stopped pestering you. Told you it would work!'

'I'm so happy for you, Mondo,' Portia said, sounding relieved. 'Can we go tell everyone else the truth now? I didn't enjoy lying to the pixies!'

'But you did a great job,' Grace laughed. 'Giant slugs? How'd you dream that one up?!'

Portia shrugged. 'I read an awful lot of books.'

Grace laughed. Questival was finally feeling like fun, and she didn't even care about winning the Golden Plume any more.

Well, maybe just a *teensy-weensy* bit.

14

DO NOT ALERT
THE LEADERS

Grace hadn't had a wink of sleep or a single slice of toast for breakfast, but she didn't care. With the pixies gone, she also had no distractions.

Instead of constantly keeping their eyes on the Pixies' Pick, the other competitors had turned *their* focus to questing now, too. Sure, they enjoyed watching Mondo's floating tools and weapons **SWISHING, BIFFING** and **TWIRLING** through the air – but they were too busy topping up their own scores to waste time staring.

The leader board was constantly changing as the young knights dug deep, doing their best to complete each task.

'It's so much easier to concentrate without all that singing,' said Grace, striding fearlessly over molten lava in the fire-walking arena.

'I hope the pixies are OK,' said Portia, following her with a dainty hop, skip and a jump. They're missing all the action!'

'Oh, they'll be SUPER DUPER happy in Giant Country,' said Mondo breezily. 'We have our own pixie population there, too.'

'Fascinating,' said Portia.

'Don't they get on your nerves?' asked Grace.

'Nah,' said Mondo. 'The place is so huge we hardly ever see each other. Here goes – it's my turn to toast my tootsies ...'

Her huge footprints were briefly visible as she made her way across the lava. 'Nailed it!' she whooped.

Grace smiled. Her new friend's confidence was no longer an act. It seemed being invisible was allowing Mondo to relax and be herself. Sir Oliver and Sir Arthur applauded. 'Bravo, Mondo!'

'Keep it down,' said Portia. 'The pixies might hear you and come back!'

'Not a chance,' said Sir Oliver, stepping gingerly across the lava. 'I expect they'll be singing most vexatious songs to all those giant slugs.'

'There *are* no slugs, remember?' Grace said, skipping across the lava a second time, just for fun. 'We made them up to get rid of the pixies.'

The tips of Sir Arthur's ears turned pink. 'We knew that,' he said, giving Sir Oliver a sideways look.

'No slugs, got it,' Sir Oliver said, a little too eagerly. 'We only told a few people about them anyhow.'

Portia rolled her eyes. 'Who did you tell?'

'No one special,' said Sir Arthur quickly. He'd just completed the quest, too, and his socks were smoking. 'Besides, everyone knows there's no such thing as giant slugs.'

'Enough slug talk,' Mondo said. 'Let's go SMASH another quest!'

Grace rubbed her hands together eagerly. 'How about maze-solving next?'

'LET'S GO!' yelled Mondo.

Grace burst out laughing as she and Portia were grabbed by invisible hands and tugged towards the arena.

♪ ♫ ♪

The morning flew by as they completed one quest after another.

Hex-breaking!

Cave-sneaking!

Frog-flipping!

Pulling-swords-from-stones!

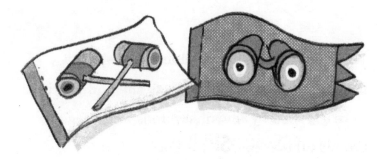

By mid-afternoon the girls had ticked off every single quest.

'What time is it?' asked Portia. 'Can we have one last go at something before Questival ends?'

Mondo's invisible stomach growled loudly. 'Excuse me,' she said.

'I'm hungry, too,' said Grace, grinning. 'How about a spot of airborne lunch ... ?'

The girls headed for the food-fighting arena. It was jam-packed with ravenous knights, finishing Questival in deliciously messy style.

'I think this might be my MOST

FAVOURITEST quest,' Mondo announced, picking up a cream pie in each hand.

Grace ducked as the pies flew through the air and **SMOOSHED** Portia on the nose.

SPLAT! SPLOT!

'In your FACE, Portia!' Mondo chuckled.

Portia didn't even flinch. She picked up two custard cakes, launching one at her friend, and another at her sister. 'Take *that*!'

Grace caught a cake in the face, but Mondo dodged every missile. 'Not fair!' Portia said. 'We can't see what we're aiming at!'

'This is the best day of my life!' Grace said, catching a stray toffee tart in mid-air and taking a bite.

'Mine too,' Portia agreed.

'Questival is the absolute TIPPY TOPS!'
said Mondo, juggling three pies in her unseen
hands.

'Look!' said Portia, pointing to Questival's
main gates. 'Everyone's friends and family
are beginning to arrive. The Golden Plume
Ceremony must be starting soon.'

Grace turned her gaze across the campsite.
A steady trickle of visitors were making their
way to the presentation arena.

'Blistering boggart butts!' Grace grumbled.

'I don't want it to end!'

'D'you think there's time to do pin-the-tail-on-the-stick-man again?' Portia begged. 'It took me four goes before. I kept picking out actual twigs by mistake.'

'Let's do it!' Grace grinned, grabbing a flying cookie on her way out.

Even though Mondo went unseen, her skill at finding stick men was crystal clear. In the time it took Grace and Portia to find just *one* of them, the invisible giant had successfully spotted *seven*.

'I wish I could do it that quickly,' Portia sighed in frustration. 'How are you so good at this, Mondo?'

'My ears are ASTRONOMICAL,' Mondo answered honestly. 'I can hear their *teensy-weensy* footsteps rustling in the leaves. Listen hard and try again.'

Portia put her ear to the ground. 'Oh, wow, you're right! OK, here goes ...'

Grace watched, impressed, as her sister zoned in on a seemingly empty spot on the ground and then snatched up what looked like an ordinary branch.

'Oh, no you don't!' said Portia, setting the stick on the ground. 'There! Off you go!'

The branch stuck out two little legs

and scurried back into the brush pile.

'Smashed it!' said Portia triumphantly. 'Thanks for the advice, Mondo.'

'You can't see, but I'm doing a MAHOOSIVE smile,' said Mondo.

'Questival's *way* more exciting now everyone's doing so well,' Grace said, giving her friends a *mahoosive* smile of her own. 'Anyone could win, and you know what? I don't even mind if it's not me!'

'Everyone else is already in the presentation arena,' Portia said. 'We'd better go and take our seats.'

'I have an ITTY-BITTY question first,' said Mondo. 'What has a beard, a crown and a face like thunder?'

Grace frowned. 'Is this some kind of bonus riddle-solving quest?'

'Whatever it is,' said Mondo darkly, 'it's on the horizon and it's coming this way.'

Portia turned her gaze to the hills and groaned. 'Oh, no – it's Dad!'

'It looks like he's heading for Giant Country,' said Mondo.

'What's he doing *that* for?' Grace said, appalled.

'Er,' said Sir Oliver, popping up behind them sheepishly with Sir Arthur, 'he might have heard something about those giant slugs …'

'You said you didn't tell anyone important?!' said Portia.

Grace's jaw dropped open in horror. 'You told our *dad*?!'

'Of course not,' said Sir Arthur, blushing. 'We told Ross Rigglebottom, and HE told your dad.'

'We're sorry!' said Sir Oliver quickly. 'We were only doing our duty!'

Mondo groaned. 'If your DINKY DAD tells Mum I've left Questival, she'll be furious!'

Portia gulped. 'What'll she do?'

'She'll come straight here to look for me, **GUARANTEEKED**. I'm supposed to be showing off my skills as a STUPENDOUS FUTURE LEADER and winning the Golden Plume, not hiding away!'

'You could reverse the magic?' Portia suggested. 'If your mum turns up, she'll soon calm down when she sees you're here.'

Mondo began, 'Spell be done—'

'STOP!' said Grace, 'It's too risky. You heard what Verity said. The potion will wear off by itself soon enough, but reversing the magic could change you forever. Portia and I are just going to have to stop him,' Grace decided firmly.

'I'll come, too,' said Mondo. 'I want to help, even if just a TEENY bit!'

'You'll be the biggest help if you keep a low profile,' Grace said, wishing she could look Mondo in the eye. 'I don't think Dad will be too happy if he finds out what we've been up to.'

'Grace is right,' said Portia. 'If you thought the *pixies* were giving you unwanted attention, just wait until you see what our dad's capable of.'

Grace hoped Mondo wouldn't have to find out. She hurried off to find Poop. She had to stop her father, fast.

15

NEVER LIE TO
YOUR PARENTS

Grace and Portia dashed to the marshmallow glade, leaped on to their unicorns and headed out to intercept their father.

… Slowly.

Poop and Sprinkles had spent most of the past two days gorging on marshmallows.

'You're like a pair of giant slugs yourselves,' Grace tutted as they plodded

out of the campsite.

Grace's heart fell as she saw that her father was riding Julio Splendido. Julio was the fastest steed in the royal stables. He treated every outing like it was a race. 'We'll never catch them!' said Portia.

But Grace had spotted something that gave her hope. 'We have a chance – Taffy's in the saddle, too!'

Their tutor was seated behind the king, furry arms wrapped tightly around his waist.

The extra weight was definitely slowing Julio Splendido down. Poop and Sprinkles had begun to find their stride. The girls were catching up.

'Hey, Dad!' Grace called, once their father was within hearing distance. 'Wait for us!'

Julio Splendido seemed annoyed at having to stop, but King Wonder and his passenger looked a little relieved. 'You don't have to hold on *quite* so tightly, Taffy,' King Wonder said, prising the troll's fingers apart.

'I'm s-sorry, your majesty!' Taffy said, eyes wide and unblinking. 'I'm not used to such s-speed!'

'Hi!' Grace said cheerfully. 'You do realise you just missed the turning for the campsite?'

'We're not *going* to the campsite,' King Wonder said gravely.

'You ought to be,' Grace said. 'The Golden Plume Ceremony will be starting any minute, and you have to present the Golden Plume to the winner.'

'We're not sure who's won,' said Portia. 'We're waiting for the final score to be announced.'

'I'm afraid you'll have to wait a bit longer,' Taffy squeaked. 'There are giant slugs to tackle!'

'Giant slugs?!' Grace laughed, slapping her thigh. 'Good one!'

'This is no laughing matter,' said the king gravely. 'Giant Country is under attack!'

'I'm surprised you're not headed there yourselves,' said Taffy. 'Ross Rigglebottom said Chief Colossa's daughter dropped everything to go and help!'

'He must've got the wrong end of the

mallet,' Portia said.

Taffy pulled a scroll out from his waistcoat, unfurled it and read it aloud. *"I have been reliably informed by Sirs Oliver and Arthur that Mondo Colossa has left Questival to tackle giant slugs in Giant Country."*

Portia shot Grace a worried look.

'No chance,' Grace said matter-of-factly. 'Mondo's a friend of ours. If she was in Giant Country, we'd know about it. Plus there's no such thing as giant slugs. Right, Portia?'

'Er, yeah?'

'They were probably talking about Mondo's giant *glugs*,' Grace continued. 'I'm not surprised they thought it was worth contacting you. She was *beyond impressive* in the hot-chocolate-chugging quest.'

'I know, right?' said Portia, catching on.

'I only managed three mugs, but Mondo drank the whole vat!'

'Mondo's at Questival right now, waiting to find out who won the Golden Plume,' said Grace. 'She's been an amazing competitor. I'm pretty sure she'll win ...'

'EEEP!' The gap between Grace and Portia gasped excitedly. The girls shared an urgent look.

Taffy's fur stood on end, while the king's eyebrows shot up his forehead and disappeared beneath his crown.

'SLUG!' shrieked Taffy, sticking his head under the king's robe in an attempt to hide.

King Wonder drew his mallet from his belt and looked frantically around for whatever had made the noise. 'Show yourself, you foul, slimy whopper!'

Grace sighed heavily. 'Put your mallet down, Dad. You won't be needing it.'

The king narrowed his eyes, but he didn't lower his mallet. 'Why do I get the feeling you two are up to something?'

'Dad and Taffy,' said Grace, holding out a hand to indicate the space where Mondo stood. 'Meet Mondo Colossa.'

Taffy peeped out from beneath the king's robe and frowned. '*Where?*'

'Nice to meet you, your TEENSY-WEENSY majesty,' boomed Mondo, startling the king so much his crown fell off. 'Oopsies!'

Taffy's ears drooped. 'W-what in all Wonder … ?!'

Grace groaned. 'So much for trying to keep a low profile.'

The king watched, open-mouthed, as his

crown floated up off the ground and hovered right back on to his head. 'But, who? But ... what? But ... *how*?!' the king spluttered, examining the crown for hidden strings.

'We told you.' Grace shrugged. 'Mondo *never left Questival*. She's standing right beside you.'

Her father pulled himself together, straightened up in the saddle and glared down his nose at her. 'What in all Wonder have you been up to this time?!'

16

DO NOT LEAD
YOUR FRIENDS ASTRAY

'Explain yourself, Grace Wonder,' the king
fumed. 'Why is the future Chief of the Giants
invisible?!'

Grace knew she had a lot of explaining
to do; she just wasn't sure where to begin.
Thankfully, she didn't have to.

'*I* can explain, your majesty,' said Mondo.
She lifted Taffy gently out of the saddle

and cradled him in her arms.

'P-please put me down!' the old troll squeaked. 'I don't like heights!'

Mondo set Taffy back down on the ground. He immediately scurried to hide between Julio Splendido's legs. 'Sorry, hairy cutie,' said Mondo.

At any other time, Grace might have laughed, but the look on her father's face told her not to.

'I'm waiting,' he said crossly.

'The pixies wouldn't leave me alone,' said Mondo sadly. 'They were making questing *so hard.*'

'It's true,' said Portia. 'They were really upsetting her!'

'We tried other ways of getting rid of them,' Grace added. 'But pretending

Mondo had gone home was the only one that worked.'

'Why would anyone want to get rid of the pixies?!' said Taffy. 'It's an honour to be picked by them!'

'I know,' Mondo said quietly. 'But it's a nuisance, too. Especially when you don't like attention.'

'Mondo's really shy,' Grace added.

'Shy or not, your mother will certainly be giving you some attention when she finds out you've done a disappearing act,' said King Wonder sternly.

'Please don't tell her,' Mondo begged. 'She wants me to show off my leadership skills. She'll be HUMONGOUSLY disappointed in me if she thinks I'm hiding away!'

'You didn't do this alone,' the king said,

glaring at his daughters. 'My girls clearly had a hand in it.'

'You wanted everyone to be able to enjoy Questival,' Grace said. 'We were just trying to help.'

Taffy tugged anxiously at his long ears. 'How is putting the whole realm on giant slug alert *helpful*?!'

'No harm's been done,' Portia said. 'Now Mondo's invisible, everyone's having a great time, just like you hoped!'

'I don't think Chief Colossa will be very happy about this ...' said King Wonder anxiously.

'Chief Colossa doesn't even need to know!' Grace said. 'Mondo will reappear as soon as the potion wears off. Old Mother Merriwinkle said —'

Her father **ERUPTED**. 'I should've *known* those witches had something to do with this!' he roared. 'Dabbling in magic is dangerous!'

'I was never in any danger,' said Mondo firmly. 'I'm big enough to make my own decisions, and you know what I've decided? Your daughters are the most **COLOSSALLY AWESOME** friends I've ever made.'

King Wonder raised an eyebrow at Grace. 'I thought you said she was shy?'

'She seems pretty bold to me,' said Taffy, venturing out from beneath the unicorn.

'I'm feeling much braver thanks to Grace and Portia,' Mondo said. 'When I first got to Questival, I was just *acting* confident. I don't have to pretend any more. I'm having the most GIGANTEROUS fun. Thanks for making Questival open to all.'

King Wonder sighed so heavily he almost seemed to deflate. 'You're welcome,' he said with a bow. 'Let's just hope you reappear before your mother sees you.'

'Or *doesn't* see me,' said Mondo.

'With any luck, she'll never know you drank that potion,' said Grace.

'A little luck would be great right now,'

Portia joked. 'Where's a dragon when you need one?!'

'Actually,' said Taffy, gazing hopefully at the sky. 'I believe I hear wingbeats ...'

'That's not a dragon,' groaned Grace.

'Oh, no!' said Mondo. 'The lickle pickles are back!'

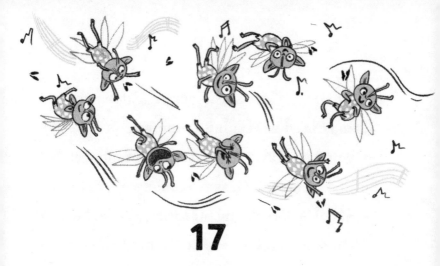

17

DO NOT CROSS
CHIEF COLOSSA

Grace could hardly believe what she was seeing. All the way to the horizon, the sky was an unnatural shade of bright, buzzy blue.

One after another the pixies came, searching high and low, calling desperately for Mondo. Grace held her breath as one flew right up to her and lifted her helmet to look underneath.

'Mondo … ?' it asked, looking extremely disappointed when all it found was unbrushed hair and a stray toast crust. 'No Mondo!' it howled, dropping Grace's helmet with a **CLANG!** before flying off to search the bushes.

'I'm sure there weren't this many of them before,' Grace said.

'They must have met up with the others in Giant Country,' Mondo said, keeping her voice low so as not to alert them to her presence.

'Perhaps it's a good sign?' Portia said hopefully.

'A *good sign*?' said King Wonder furiously. 'Your actions have caused a major swarm! Wondermere hasn't seen one of those since —'

'Since the Dull Ages!' said Taffy, still cowering beneath Julio Splendido. 'It was dreadful!'

'*How* dreadful?' Grace asked, not really wanting to hear any more details.

'Wondermere's entire pixie population became terribly agitated when their favourite ogre went into early hibernation,' Taffy said, dashing back to hide under Julio's broad belly. 'They got into a panic and drove the whole realm to distraction trying to wake it. Do you *know* how hard it is to wake an ogre?'

Grace shrugged. 'It can't be *that* hard.'

'It's IMPOSSIBLE,' her father snapped. 'The ogre slept for *three years*, and those pixies sang the whole time!'

'Oh,' said Portia quietly.

'I guess they hadn't invented ear stoppers in the Dull Ages,' Grace said.

Her father scowled at her. 'Ear stoppers were no use *then*, and they'll be no use *now*.

When pixies panic, *everyone* panics. It's contagious!'

'This is terrible!' Portia groaned.

'It certainly will be once they reach the Pixie Pastures,' said King Wonder. 'We'll have a mass panic on our hands before you know it!'

Grace gazed anxiously towards the campsite, where the pixies were massing in an enormous blue thundercloud.

'We have to stop them,' said Mondo boldly.

'It's not possible,' said King Wonder, exasperated.

'Maybe not, but we have to try,' said Mondo firmly. 'Who's with me?'

'Right beside you,' said Grace, flipping down the visor on her helmet.

Thankfully, both Poop and Sprinkles seemed to understand the urgency of the situation. They pulled in their bellies, picked up the pace and thundered back towards the campsite.

Thinking it was a race, Julio Splendido followed close behind, with King Wonder grasping for the reins and swinging a green-looking Taffy back into the saddle. The troll clung on for dear life.

As they neared the gates, Grace began to think her father was right. Maybe stopping the pixies really was impossible? It certainly looked that way.

The wild, blue swarm was **ZZZZIPPING** through every tent, backpack, sleeping bag, can of beans and suit of armour. One pixie stopped in mid-air, swivelled its antennae in their direction, then flew right past them, making a beeline for the king.

'Look out!' Grace cried, trying to shield him. It was no use. The little critter shot up the king's sleeve and began rummaging around beneath his robes.

'WHERE GO MONDO?!' it wailed.

'There's a pixie in my Under-Wonders!' the king cried, giggling uncontrollably. 'Get it out, it tickles!'

'I'll save you, sire,' cried Taffy, grabbing the king's waistband and pulling his trousers down around his ankles.

The pixie flew out, flapping frantically into Grace's face. 'WHERE GO MONDO?' it repeated miserably.

Grace looked around. Where *was* Mondo? For the briefest of moments, she wondered if perhaps Mondo had given up and run away. She certainly wouldn't have blamed her.

But they were a team, and teams stuck together. The giant's voice boomed out, loud and proud.

'COO-EE! I'M RIGHT HERE, LICKLE PICKLES!'

The pixie fell silent. Its antennae twitched. It frowned in confusion, blinked, then shook its fist at Grace. 'She is lying! Sneaky Grace!' it said angrily. 'There's no Mondo in this place!'

'NO MONDOOOOO!' wailed another pixie

at top volume, causing several others to take up the cry.

'NOOOOOO MONDOOOOOOOO!'

they chorused, tearing apart tent after tent in search of their missing winner.

'I'M RIGHT HERE!' Mondo yelled. But it was no use. Even at top volume, Mondo's voice was no match for the pixies' painfully catchy song.

'GRACE CAN'T TRICK US! SHE'S SO BAD!

MONDO'S GONE AND WE'RE ALL SAD!
GRACE MADE MONDO GO FROM HERE!
WE'LL SING SAD SONGS TIL NEXT
YEAR!'

'We've ruined Questival!' groaned Portia.

Grace had to admit, it certainly looked
that way. Stray arrows, mallets and welly
boots were flying in all directions. Every
knight and troll was being tickled, searched
and pulled in the pixies' positively
painstaking search for their champion.

The sense of panic really was contagious.

'Heeeeelp!' wailed Ross Rigglebottom, running past with a pixie dive-bombing his head. The other knight's unicorns were stampeding in alarm and confusion, trampling tents in their bid to flee from the agitated swarm.

'The lickle pickles won't believe I'm here until they can see me,' Mondo said. 'I have to reverse the spell!'

Grace turned to face her friend. 'Are you sure, Mondo?' she asked grimly.

Portia looked wretched. 'But it's so risky,' she said, wringing her hands together.

'It has to be worth a try,' said Grace. 'I mean, at least things can't get much worse.'

'Oh, yes they can,' said Portia, her voice high with anxiety. 'Here comes Mondo's mum!'

18

ALWAYS FOLLOW
THE LEADER

Grace froze. She *had* heard some heavy
THUDDING, but she'd assumed it was the
pounding of her own heart. Now she caught
sight of Mondo's GIGANTIC mother.

If Mondo was a giant, Chief Colossa was
a TITAN. She strode heavily into Questival,
kicking through collapsed tents as if they
were nothing more than fallen leaves.

She came to a standstill in front of the girls, planting herself firmly on the spot. She reminded Grace of Mondo when she'd first arrived at camp – hands on hips, chin up and gaze firmly down. Mondo had only been *acting* confident, but there could be no doubting Chief Colossa was the real deal.

Grace gulped. It didn't matter that Chief Colossa had left Giant Country without removing her hair curlers. She was super intimidating.

The huge woman slowly turned her

gaze from left to right, scanning the scene at her feet for signs of her daughter. Grace swallowed hard as the Chief of the Giants fixed her with a penetrating stare.

'WHERE'S MY DAUGHTER?' she bellowed. 'AND WHO IS TO ANSWER FOR THIS CHAOS?'

'Colossa, my old chum,' King Wonder began, trotting over on Julio Splendido. 'I can explain if you'd just calm down ...'

'CALM DOWN?!' she roared, glaring down her nose at him.

'MY DAUGHTER'S GONE MISSING, AND YOU EXPECT ME TO BE CALM?!'

Grace gulped. Being told off by King Wonder was *never* as bad as this! She could only *begin* to imagine how bad Mondo must be feeling.

'Strictly speaking, that's not exactly true …' Taffy began.

Chief Colossa turned her blistering gaze on the troll. 'Let me tell you what ALSO isn't true,' she said, bending down and looking him straight in the eye. 'It ISN'T TRUE that my country is being overrun by SLUGS, and it CERTAINLY isn't true that Mondo has come home to help deal with them!'

'Ah,' said King Wonder, fiddling nervously with the hem of his robe. 'Quite right, Colossa, well spotted.'

'So where IS she? She's meant to be SHOWING OFF her leadership skills to your whole disorderly realm!'

Grace would have spoken up by now, only she was busy trying to soothe Mondo. Her friend's fingers were gripping her arm tightly.

'I'm in so much trouble!' Mondo whimpered.

Grace took a deep breath. Mondo had stood up to King Wonder earlier. Now it was *her* turn to take the lead. 'Don't worry,' Grace said, sounding more confident than she felt. 'Teams stick together.'

She prised Mondo's invisible hand from her arm, cleared her throat and stepped boldly forward.

'If you please, your honour,' Grace said firmly. 'Mondo is an incredible leader. She's certainly set an amazing example to me.'

'Me too,' said Portia, coming to stand beside Grace. 'And she's been acing Questival.'

'It's true,' Grace added, feeling a little braver with her sister by her side. 'I'm pretty sure she finished top of the leader board!'

She felt as though she were shrinking as Chief Colossa fixed her gaze on her. 'Leader-board-topping knights don't hide from their mothers. So tell me – where in all Wonder *is* this amazing daughter of mine?'

'I'm right here, Mum,' Mondo said loudly, nudging Grace and Portia apart as she stepped between them. 'And I'm *not* hiding. At least, not any more. **Spell be done,'** she said, her voice clear above the drone of the pixies. **'Kazoo! Kazam! Show me as I truly am!'**

Grace watched intently as her enormous friend began to reappear. Chief Colossa's huge eyes grew even huger as her daughter's face came into view, floating over Grace's shoulder.

'How do I look so far?' said Mondo, a little anxiously. 'Am I changed forever?'

'You look the same to me,' said Portia. 'Ooh, there are your knees!'

'What do you mean, *changed forever*?' said Chief Colossa.

'I'm afraid the Merriwinkles had a hand in this, Colossa ...' King Wonder said nervously.

'The *Merriwinkles*?' Chief Colossa's eyebrows shot skyward as she watched her daughter reappear.

'Look! There are my not-so-teensy tootsies!' said Mondo, delighted.

'That looks like all of you,' Grace said, waiting for an explosion, a spray of sparks or a hint of sprouting antlers.

'You're back!' Portia said, giving Mondo a massive hug.

'I'm not sure whether to feel angry or relieved,' said Chief Colossa, still looking furious.

'You know what? I *have* changed forever,' said Mondo firmly. 'From now on, I'll be happy to stand out – so long as I have my friends beside me.'

As if to prove the point, she strode right

up to her mother and said, 'It's time to stand up for myself!'

'Go, Mondo!' said Grace, punching the air.

'That's nice,' said Taffy fretfully. 'But Questival is still in ruins!'

Portia smiled broadly. 'It's OK! Now the pixies can see Mondo's back, everything will return to normal!'

'Over here, pixies!' Grace yelled. 'Here's your winner, the best of us all!'

A few pixies heard. They flew over, studied Mondo closely, then carried right on panicking.

'I don't understand,' said Portia, frowning. 'Mondo's back. Why won't they calm down?'

'Because,' Grace said thoughtfully. 'She's not their chosen winner!'

Her father rolled his eyes. 'Stop being so

competitive!' he said sternly. 'I *know* you want to win the Golden Plume, but you have to admit —'

Grace smiled. 'I'm not worried about winning any more! Besides, Mondo deserves it, hands down. What I *mean* is, Mondo's a different kind of leader. She wants *everyone* to enjoy the glory. Right, Mondo?'

Mondo clapped her hands together. 'Come on, everyone. It's time we *all* shared the spotlight.'

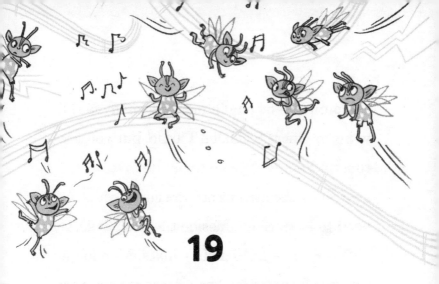

19

ALWAYS PROVIDE A PERCH FOR A PIXIE

'Well, I don't see how you can put this right,' said Chief Colossa to her daughter haughtily. 'It's your fault it's such a mess to begin with!'

'It has to be worth a try,' said Mondo.

'Teams stick together,' said Grace, taking a stand between Mondo and Portia. 'We've got your back, Mondo.'

Mondo stood firm, hands on hips. 'Listen

up, campers!' she hollered. 'We need you all to be the most STUPENDOUS leaders you can be! You don't have to be the fastest, the biggest or the strongest. You certainly don't need to be perfect. Just be the best YOU.'

'Everyone pick a pixie – just one,' shouted Grace. 'Show it why YOU deserve to win the Golden Plume!'

'GO, TEAM!' yelled Mondo, punching the air and accidentally swatting a pixie. **'OOPSIES!** Forgive me, lickle pickle, you look like you need a cuddle.'

Grace watched, smiling, as Mondo cradled her pixie gently in her huge arms. Soon it was gazing lovingly into the giant's eyes, singing softly. 'Mondo is the very best. Mondo wins the final quest!'

'This might just work,' Grace said to

Portia. 'Go pick a pixie and do your thing!'

Portia didn't need telling twice. She selected a book from one of the many she carried in her deep dress pockets, opened it up and showed it to the nearest pixie. 'Did you know that pixies have been living in these pastures since the days of Queen Wonder the Third?'

The pixie's antennae twitched. It

quietened down
and took a perch on
her shoulder, gazing
at the open pages.

'It's marvellous, really,'
Portia continued. 'Maybe
you can tell me some more
facts about yourself? I'd love
to know how you come up with those catchy
melodies ...'

The pixie began to sing, calming itself
with its own bouncy rhythm. 'Portia is so
kind and wise! She'll beat all the other guys!'

Grace watched, delighted, as the other
campers began to follow suit. 'Sir Arthur is
so nice and sweet,' sang his chosen pixie.
'He will win! He can't be beat!'

Sir Oliver was doing just as well with his

little blue buddy. It was perched on his shoulder, cheering loudly into his ear. 'Always honest, always true! Who will win? It's YOU, YOU, YOU!'

Grace felt a twinge of anxiety as she spotted Chief Colossa watching Mondo intently. Grace couldn't help but feel that she had put Mondo's relationship with her mum at risk just so *she* could come out top at Questival. What had she been thinking? That wasn't how teams worked.

But this was no time to dwell. Her own leadership might have been questionable, but Mondo's was a triumph. Right now, everyone was working together, doing their own thing as part of a team. The pixies were calming down. There was only one panicking blue pest left, flapping fretfully around her.

It was Grace's turn to help fix the damage. She took a deep breath.

'I'm not sure what to tell you,' she said, feeling suddenly unsure of her own abilities. 'When I came to Questival, I thought *I* was the best. But I'm not, unless you count being the best at messing up.'

The pixie buzzed doubtfully, but Grace carried on. 'The funny thing is, I don't even mind that I'm not going to win the Golden Plume. It's great to see my friends doing so well.'

The pixie launched itself at her face. 'Steady on!' she said, staggering. 'I'm sorry! Please don't bite me!'

But the pixie planted an enormous kiss on her nose and began to sing. 'Ace-y Grace-y! Bestest knight! Messes up, then makes it

right! Best in all of Wondermere! Bring that
Golden Plume right here!'

Grace burst out laughing. She gently
plucked the pixie from her face, gave him
a big kiss in return and sat him gently on
her shoulder. As he carried on singing,
Grace realised that the other pixies were
not only calm, they were beginning to
sing in harmony.

They weren't singing the same words —
each and every pixie was championing their
own chosen leader. But they *were* all in tune
with one another.

The pixies' new song was deeply soothing.
The site was still a mess, with tents and
camping gear strewn everywhere, but it
didn't seem to matter at all.

'Well I never,' purred Ross Rigglebottom,
while a pixie sang a catchy ditty about his
magnificent facial hair.

Grace caught Portia's eye, and then
Mondo's. The three friends grinned at one
another. 'You know, I don't think we ruined
Questival after all,' Grace said. 'We made
it much, much better!'

'IS THAT SO?'

boomed a voice behind her. Grace turned
around and found herself face-to-knee with
Chief Colossa.

Grace gulped. Even her pixie fell silent.
It was time to face the *real* music.

20

EVERYONE IS
WELCOME AT QUESTIVAL

Grace's pixie gave her a reassuring pat as she addressed Chief Colossa.

'Please don't be too cross with Mondo,' she said. 'This whole mess was my fault.'

'Mine too,' Portia said, putting an arm around her sister.

'We got into this mess as a team,' said Mondo, lifting them both off the floor in a giant hug. 'And we put it right as a team, too!'

Chief Colossa looked Mondo in the eye. 'Leaders stand out,' she said, her voice surprisingly soft and tender. 'It's what makes us strong. I see a strong leader in you, Mondo.'

But Mondo smiled and shook her head. 'We're *truly* strong when we all stand together. I want to be the kind of leader who sees everyone's strengths, and helps them find them. I didn't mean to make such a mess of it!'

But Chief Colossa smiled, then knelt down so she could look her daughter and her friends in the eye. 'I'm very proud of you. And don't worry – we all mess up sometimes, even leaders. Right, Wilberforce?'

'It's how we deal with our mistakes that sets us apart,' said King Wonder, who had a pixie in every pocket.

'For instance,' said Chief Colossa, giving Grace a wry smile, 'your father's weakness is bog-snorkelling. I'll never forget having to rescue him when *I* was at Questival.'

King Wonder's jaw dropped. **'Sir Gregory was YOU?'**

'*You* went to Questival?!' Mondo gasped.

'But *how*?' asked Grace, puzzled.

'Yeah,' said Portia, astonished. 'This is the first year giants have been allowed to take part – not to mention girls!'

'You three aren't the *only ones* with a witch for a friend, you know,' Chief Colossa said with a wink. 'Verity's grandmother and I go *way* back.'

'But Sir Gregory was perfectly visible,' said Taffy, looking baffled. 'And regular-sized, to boot!'

'Merriwinkle's Patented Shrinking Potion,' said Chief Colossa proudly. 'I was the size of a regular knight the whole weekend! I still *looked* like a girl, though, so I kept my helmet on the whole time.'

King Wonder chuckled. 'I always wondered why my opponent never showed his face! It's good to see you again, *Sir Gregory.*'

'Amazing!' breathed Portia.

Chief Colossa turned her attention back to Mondo. 'I'm so sorry I flew off the handle before. I just didn't want to see you following in *all* my footsteps. Some of them have been **MAHOOSIVE** blunders.'

'I get it,' Mondo said, smiling. 'You were

cross because you didn't want me to hide away, like you had to.'

Colossa nodded. 'I took part in disguise because I HAD to. Questival wasn't open to all in those days. It was the only way a giant girl could take part!'

'Your mother would happily have shown everyone what she was made of, if she could,' said King Wonder, a little sadly. 'I'm only sorry it's taken me so long to change the rules.'

'No biggy, Ickle King,' said Mondo, giving him a playful punch on the shoulder.

Grace laughed. 'I reckon that magic spell really *has* changed you forever,' she said. 'You're even more awesome than before!'

Chief Colossa pulled her daughter in for a giant hug, then a pixie settled on the

Chief's enormous shoulder and began to sing. 'Chief Colossa! Mega mother! She loves Mondo like no other! Fierce protector! Constant champ! Biggest fan in this whole camp!'

'Does this mean I'm not grounded?' Mondo asked.

'Oh, no, you're absolutely grounded,' her mum chuckled.

'Us too?' Grace asked her father.

'Very much so,' said the king. 'But I think we should all squeeze in a few last quests first.'

'I'm afraid the official quests have already closed, sire,' said Ross Rigglebottom, hurrying over with his clipboard hugged tightly to his chest. Several pixies were following in his wake, trying to sneak a peek at which competitor had finished top of the leader board.

King Wonder chuckled. 'No matter! I think we should just quest for FUN.'

'Can I join in, too?' asked Chief Colossa coyly. 'I must admit, I've always wanted to come back. It would be really something to be able to compete as *myself*. That is, if I'm welcome?'

King Wonder smiled. '*Everyone* is welcome at Questival.'

'Let's send word to the Merriwinkles, Wilberforce,' said Chief Colossa. 'Perhaps they'd like to join us?'

King Wonder laughed. 'That would be *magic*,' he said.

Grace grinned. 'Last one to the bog-snorkelling arena's a giant slug!'

21

GOLDEN
WONDERS

They spent the last few hours of daylight
squeezing in as many bonus quests as
possible, each cheered on by their own
adoring pixie. Even the camp trolls joined
in, throwing themselves into each challenge
with gleeful, hairy gusto.

All too soon, it was time to call it a day.
Grace didn't mind. She'd had the time of

her life with her friends and family, sharing
in their triumphs, failures and everything
else in between.

As the first stars began to pepper the
night sky, the girls headed back to the main
arena with their fellow campers, the tireless
camp trolls, their friends and families, and
a thousand singing pixies.

'I bet you've won the Golden Plume,
Mondo,' said Grace happily.

'You really deserve it.' Portia said, giving
Mondo a hug.

'I'm not sure I do,' Mondo said. 'Either of you could easily have won it, too. You were both **RIDUNKULOUSLY** amazing!'

Grace grinned. '*Everyone* was,' she said. 'You'd never know half these campers have never tried questing before.'

'It's a doddle!' said Verity, who'd spent the evening whizzing round on her broom, completing as many quests as possible at super high speed.

'Well, I hope you're happy to take the spotlight now, Mondo?' said King Wonder quietly. 'Spoiler alert, but I've had a sneak peek at the final scores, and I ought to warn you that Ross Rigglebottom is about to pronounce you the winner.'

Grace gave her friend a concerned look. 'You don't have to stand up in front of everyone if it makes you uncomfortable.'

Mondo smiled shyly. 'I think I can handle a teensy bit of attention.'

'That's my girl,' said Chief Colossa, putting her arm around her daughter.

Ross Rigglebottom made his way up on to the stage. 'Good evening, everyone,' he announced, stroking his moustache thoughtfully. 'Sorry for the, er, slight disruption earlier tonight. We are very happy to welcome you here, and we thank the residents of Pixie Pastures for allowing us to camp in their beautiful home.'

The pixies, each sitting on or hovering near their chosen champion, stopped what they were doing to sing together as one. 'We're so glad to have you here! Please come back again next year!'

'I think it would be fair to say we've *all* found this year extra challenging,' Ross continued. 'Campers, you should be extremely proud of yourselves. You've completed every single quest, including the toughest one of all – learning to live and work together, embracing your differences.'

'Go, team!' cried Grace, throwing a double air punch.

Ross cleared his throat and continued. 'Your majesty, would you please join me on stage for the presentation of the Golden Plume?'

The whole arena seemed to hold its breath as the king joined the troll on stage and lifted the Plume from its special plinth.

'This has been an exceptional Questival,' King Wonder said. 'I'm so glad I let my daughters persuade me to do away with the old rules and make Questival open to all. Many of you arrived knowing no *one* and no *thing* about knighthood. You have done so well! But as we all know, there is one camper who has stood head and shoulders above the rest, in more ways than one. Congratulations, Mondo Colossa! Please join us on the stage and accept your trophy!'

The king smiled warmly down at Mondo. She blushed bright pink, but stayed rooted to the spot. Grace thought perhaps she felt too shy to go up after all? But then, Mondo stepped on to the stage with an easy stride. She held her head high and graciously accepted the Golden Plume from King Wonder. The crowd fell silent as she opened her mouth to speak.

'Thank you,' she said. 'I would never have thought I'd be brave enough to stand here today, in front of you all, let alone as a GREAT BIG winner. But thanks to my new friends, I've learned that I'm capable of a *lickle* bit more than I realised ...'

She beamed at Grace and Portia, who grinned back.

'Even so,' said Mondo, handing back the trophy, 'I can't accept the Golden Plume.'

The crowd gasped. The pixies twitched their antennae. King Wonder and Ross Rigglebottom shared an anxious look.

'It's not that I don't treasure it,' Mondo announced happily. 'It's just that I'm not the only one who deserves it. But don't just take my word for it – listen to the lickle pickles …'

The pixies didn't need telling twice. They broke loudly and proudly into song, quickly falling into harmony. A smile crept across Grace's face, growing wider each time she picked out a new tune.

'Ross is mega! He's my troll! He's the bestest, on the whole!'

'Wilberforce Wonder, Questival king! He's the champ of everything!'

'Taffy! Taffy! He's my man! If he can't win it, no one can!'

'Chief Colossa won before! She will win the Plume once more!'

'Mondo's better than her mum! Biff Colossa up the bum!'

Chief Colossa roared with laughter. 'EVERYONE wins the Golden Plume!'

'**EXUNKLY!**' said Mondo, holding it aloft in triumph. 'We're all **MAHOOSIVE, WHOPPING GREAT WINNERS!**'

The rest of the crowd roared with delight. Mondo wiped a happy tear from her eye. 'What a **MAG–NIF–NER–OUS** team we all make!'

'Agreed,' said King Wonder, joining Mondo as she went back to stand with the girls. 'Everyone has shown incredible leadership qualities today.'

'Even if I did need to rescue you from the

bog again,' Chief Colossa chuckled.

'Thank you, *Sir Gregory*,' said King Wonder.

'Questival rocks,' said Grace.

'Excuse me, your majesty,' said Ross Rigglebottom, 'but we only have one Golden Plume! We can't *possibly* award one to *everyone?*!'

'I'm sure a little magic can soon fix that,' said King Wonder, giving Verity a wink. 'Verity, could you please rustle up a plume for every helmet?'

'Piece of cake,' said Verity, waving her wand. In a flash, everyone's helmet sported a shimmering golden feather, with only one or two knights growing accidental antlers.

The pixies cheered and chirped in delight, hugging one another in mid-air before finally singing as one, **'EVERYBODY**

IS THE BEST–OF–ALL! HAPPY PIXIES! HAPPY QUESTIVAL!'

Grace laughed. 'It rhymes the way *they're* singing it!'

King Wonder waved to the crowd. 'May your Golden Plume always remind you of what you can achieve. We're *all* winners when we work together!'

The whole arena erupted in cheers. All apart from Grace.

'What's the matter, sweetheart?' her father asked her quietly. 'You ought to be delighted. Your open-to-all Questival is a big hit!'

'But it nearly wasn't,' Grace said. 'I caused so much trouble.'

'You helped fix it, too,' he said, pulling her into a hug. 'I'm very proud of you.'

'Even though I sometimes mess up?' Grace said quietly.

'*Especially* because of that.' Her father smiled. 'Things don't always go your way, but you never once stop trying your best. And you'll *always* be your best to me, even when you don't succeed.'

Grace hugged him back.

'We can't all be the best at everything, you know,' he said quietly. 'Take me and bog-snorkelling!'

'I can give you some tips,' she said. 'But right now, I need to practise my partying ...'

'I couldn't agree more,' King Wonder said. 'Would you care to show me how it's done?'

'Let's do this,' Grace grinned.

'Best Questival ever!'

Have you discovered Grace's first epic adventure?

DO NOT DISTURB THE DRAGONS

Seriously, don't do it. The dragons bring us
luck. We can't risk them flying away!

In fact, no breaking any rules AT ALL.
Just in case. So ... DO NOT EAT ICE CREAM
FOR BREAKFAST, OK? And NEVER STAND AT
THE WRONG END OF A UNICORN.

Oh, and if you're a girl DON'T EVEN
THINK ABOUT BECOMING A KNIGHT.
That means you, Princess Grace ...